Milo March is a hard g, James-Bondian charact[...] a combination of personal [...], and intellect. He is a sh[...] [...]uman character, a crack shot, and a deeper character than I have found in most of the other spy/thriller novels I've read. But, above all, he is a con-man—and a very good one. It is Milo March himself who makes the series worth reading.

—Don Miller, *The Mystery Nook* fanzine 12

Steeger Books is proud to reissue twenty-three vintage novels and stories by M.E. Chaber, whose Milo March Mysteries deliver mile-a-minute action and breezily readable entertainment for thriller buffs.

Milo is an Insurance Investigator who takes on the tough cases. Organized crime, grand theft, arson, suspicious disappearances, murders, and millions and millions of dollars—whatever it is, Milo is just the man for the job. Or even the only man for it.

During World War II, Milo was assigned to the OSS and later the CIA. Now in the Army Reserves, with the rank of Major, he is recalled for special jobs behind the Iron Curtain. As an agent, he chops necks, trusses men like chickens to steal their uniforms, shoots point blank at secret police—yet shows compassion to an agent from the other side.

Whatever Milo does, he knows how to do it right. When the work is completed, he returns to his favorite things: women, booze, and good food, more or less in that order....

THE MILO MARCH MYSTERIES

Green Grow the Graves

KENDELL FOSTER CROSSEN
Writing as
M.E. CHABER

With an Afterword by
KENDRA CROSSEN BURROUGHS

STEEGER BOOKS / 2021

PUBLISHED BY STEEGER BOOKS
Visit steegerbooks.com for more books like this.

PUBLISHING HISTORY

Hardcover
New York: Holt, Rinehart & Winston (A Rinehart Suspense Novel), February 1970. Dust jacket by Stan Zagorski.
Toronto: Holt, Rinehart & Winston of Canada, February 1970.
London: Robert Hale, April 1971.

Paperback
New York: Paperback Library (63-568), A Milo March Mystery, #19, April 1971. Cover by Robert McGinnis.

ISBN: 978-1-61827-581-3

For Bo—
who is more Bojangles than Beauregards,
and for Melody—
who is one.

CONTENTS

This is the story of two men who never met and had nothing in common yet were wedded together in a bloody pageantry of puppets, neither of them aware of the invisible figures who were back of the stage pulling the strings. All characters portrayed in this novel are fictional and are not meant to represent anyone living or dead. Only the climate of violence is real in a world which has seen too much of it over the centuries.

M.E.C.

ONE

It was a warm day in Cleveland, Ohio. Most of the men who had gathered in the park for the political picnic wore sport shirts and no jackets. Their wives wore light summer dresses. The men on the platform, however, wore jackets and ties, pretending they felt comfortable.

Portable ovens stood around the tables, keeping the food hot, while white-jacketed servers waited to put the food on the tables the minute the speakers were through.

It was a friendly crowd, applauding in the right places and laughing at the familiar jokes, although now and then a few of the men would glance wistfully at the ovens. A few beers would have helped them wait, but there were only soft drinks. As one man said in an undertone to the man next to him, "You can't drink much of this stuff before it starts coming out of your ears." His neighbor nodded and grinned in appreciation.

There were five men on the platform. Four were local politicians and one was from a neighboring state. Four were there to help the local man who sat in the center. He was running in a special election for the United States Senate, and it was generally agreed that he needed help. The crowd had already heard two speakers, and the third seemed about to finish.

"... and we all know," he said, "with what unswerving

courage and faithfulness Jerry Hayes has served the people of Ohio during his long political life, and I know he will continue to do so as long as there is a breath left in his body. It is in trying times such as we now face that we need men like Jerry Hayes down there in the United States Senate. Once we have put him there, we can be sure that every minute of every day he will be doing his best for the great state of Ohio and for the United States of America." He stopped and took a drink of water from a glass on the lectern in front of him. He put the glass down and looked at the audience.

"And now," he continued, "I want you to meet a man who has worked closely with Jerry Hayes, knows his ability and integrity, knows his contributions and his sacrifices for his state and country. You know the man I'm about to introduce to you. You know him well. You've listened to him on radio, watched him on television, and read his speeches in the newspapers until you probably feel that you have known him all of your lives even though he does not come from Ohio but from one of our great neighboring states. I give you the Honorable John Randolph."

There was considerable applause as the man seated at the end stood up and came to the center of the platform. He was a tall, handsome man, no more than forty, although his wavy hair was already quite gray at the temples. He was well dressed and the only one there who seemed not to mind the heat. As he reached the lectern, he held up his hands to stop the applause.

"My friends," he said, "—and I have many friends in this great state—my only regret is that I can't spend more time here so that I could get to know more of you. That, as you must know, is one of the wonderful things about being in political life. We make so many, many friends. Of course, we make a few enemies, too."

As he waited for them to laugh, smiling back at them, one realized how often his handsome face had been seen on television or in the pages of the newspaper, how many times that mellow voice had been heard on radio, television, and at meetings such as this. It was impossible not to wonder, as his colleagues did constantly, what he wanted. It was said that he traveled more than anyone in Congress, making speeches wherever he was wanted or wherever they would have him. The networks knew that he could be counted on to appear on television even if asked at the last minute. Did he want to move from the House to the Senate? Or did his desires go further than that?

"I am going to talk to you today," he went on, "not about politics but about America and Americans. That is the kind of talk Jerry Hayes understands and appreciates. He knows, and I know, that we need more of that kind of talk in both the lower and upper houses. We need men who are not afraid to talk about America and Americans."

He stopped again and there was applause.

"You know me," he cried. "John Randolph. There has been a Randolph in every generation in public service since the first Randolph in the very beginning of this nation. My ancestors owned black slaves. They also owned some white people who weren't much better than slaves. They couldn't quit working for us unless we said they could. But we were a poor nation, just beginning then. Now we're the richest and the strongest and the greatest nation in the world. I say let every American who wants to be an American share in this wonderful country.

"Of course, they have to earn their share just like I did and you did. But they've got to have the right to do it. We can't hand it to them on a silver platter, but we can see that they have the right to get an education and to get the same jobs that you and I get. And they've got the right to get the same salary, and we have to see that they get it. When we do that, they won't have to pay a lot of money to some union to tell them what to do and when to do it, some union that will tell them to go out on strike and make them lose more in wages than they'll get in any raise.

"If I didn't believe in America for Americans, whether they're black or white or green, and if I didn't fight for that belief, what do you think would happen when I go up to meet my Maker? All those Randolphs who helped to set up this country so it could grow the way it has, they'd just look at me and want to know what I was doing there. And about all I could say was that I had spent most of my life in the Lower House and that I thought maybe I'd get a chance to sit in the Upper House."

While the audience laughed, one of the men sitting on the platform leaned over to the man next to him. "Sometimes," he said, "I can't tell whether it's Jerry or Randolph who's running for the Senate."

"A moment ago," Randolph continued, "another speaker told you that Ohio needed Jerry Hayes down in Washington. I say amen to that. I also say that Washington needs Jerry down there. We need all the men like Jerry Hayes we can find."

This time the applause was loud. Randolph waited with a friendly smile until it died out.

"I sat," he said, "in the House with Jerry Hayes for six years. He worked with me on civil rights bills, on urban renewal bills, on antipollution bills, on anticrime bills to make the streets safe for our women and children, on anti-Communist bills, on bills to curb the power—and the abuse of that power—of unions. And I can stand here and tell you that there was never a finer man to work with than Jerry—"

It sounded like a firecracker. So much so that several people looked toward the street to see if there were any children playing there.

When they looked back, the first thing they saw was the blood streaming down the speaker's face. Before the meaning of it could sink in, Randolph leaned forward as though he were bowing to the audience. Then, swiftly, he fell from the platform, taking the lectern and the microphone with him.

A woman screamed like a high-pitched trumpet.

TWO

The morning was hot and sticky in New York City. I was sitting in my office with my coat off, my feet up on the desk, reading the morning newspaper. Almost a month had passed since the assassination of Congressman John Randolph, but he was still making the front pages almost every day. Most of it wasn't really news, but it was the absence of news that made the papers.

They thought they'd identified the man who shot Randolph. They said his name was Eugene Crown and that he was a convict who had escaped from prison only a few weeks before the killing. They claimed to have found the murder rifle with his prints on it and to have found his car abandoned in Akron, Ohio. The police of every city and every state were working on it. So were the FBI. Nobody seemed to have any idea why he'd shot Randolph. And they didn't have Crown. He'd been reported seen in Los Angeles, Flagstaff, St. Louis, Memphis, Atlanta, Newark, and New York City. But that's all they had. Reports.

There was also an editorial, I think the tenth I'd seen, about what it was doing to our image in Europe. This was our fourth political assassination—fifth if you counted the killing of the man accused of committing one of them—in less than six years. Finally, I turned to the sports page.

I am Milo March. My office is on Madison Avenue in New York City. I have a license which says I am a private detective, although I'm actually an insurance investigator. A specialist. At least, that's what I call myself when I tell the insurance companies how much I'm going to charge them. But at the moment I was an unemployed insurance investigator. I still had some money from my last job, but I was getting tired of hanging around the office. Maybe, I thought, it would be a good idea to go to some nice place with air-conditioning—like a bar, for example—when the phone rang.

I scooped it up and said hello.

"Milo, my boy, how are you?" a familiar voice said. It was Martin Raymond, vice-president of Intercontinental Insurance. I do most of my work for them.

"I'm not sure," I said. "Nobody's asked me until now."

He gave his automatic laugh, which was supposed to signify that he knew a joke when he heard it. The truth of the matter was that he didn't.

"Are you busy?" he asked.

"Nothing so busy that it would make a crash if I dropped it. Are you just making idle conversation, or do you have a job for me?" I knew he never made idle conversation.

"There might be something," he said. He sounded different than usual. "I thought we might have lunch together and discuss it."

"You can't buy me for a luncheon. When and where?"

"I thought we might go to the Club. Suppose you meet me there in an hour? It's nice and quiet there and we can talk."

The Club was a place where he went to play handball. I

don't know how nice a place it is, but it certainly is quiet. "I'll be there," I said, and hung up.

I finished reading the paper and then went down to get a cab, timing it so I'd be a few minutes late. Martin Raymond was already there, glancing at his watch, when I entered the dining room. He didn't like people to be late. Time and money and all that sort of thing.

"A bit late, aren't you?" he said as I sat down.

"Yeah. The dogs got in a traffic jam."

"Dogs?"

I nodded. "I always take a dog sled. Much faster than a taxi. Doesn't everyone?"

"Oh." He gave a short laugh, but his heart wasn't in it. "Care for a drink?"

"I thought you'd never ask me."

He beckoned the waiter over and ordered a manhattan. I ordered a dry martini. Nothing was said until the drinks came. I lifted my glass.

"To dear old Intercontinental," I said. "I gather that someone is trying to dip their greedy little fingers into the family till."

"No. Nothing like that. Not that we know about, at least."

That was strange, I thought. As long as I'd known Martin Raymond, he had never asked me to come to the office or taken me out to lunch unless Intercontinental had a case of insurance fraud on their hands.

"Well," I said lightly, "if this is just to buy me a farewell lunch, skip it. I'd rather have the gold watch and the touching speeches by the members of the board. On second thought, we can forget the speeches."

He took another swallow of his drink and frowned. "As a matter of fact, this is a little unusual. And it was the board of directors that suggested you be hired. But it is not insurance fraud. In fact, we're paying the claim promptly without any question."

"Now I've heard everything," I said. "What happened? Did the chairman get mixed up in a little badger game or something like that?"

He finished his drink, caught the waiter's attention, and motioned for two more drinks for us. That was a bit unusual, too. Normally he would have one cocktail and then dive into the food.

He waited until the drinks came. "This is a serious moment in the life of Intercontinental Insurance," he said. It must have been serious if he was going to ignore my levity. He also sounded as if he were going to make a speech. I held on to my martini and prepared for the worst. "Intercontinental is about to take a step which I do not believe has ever been taken by any other insurance company." He meditated over his drink.

"If you are going to take a step," I said, "the first thing to do is to lift one foot."

He frowned. "Yes. Of course, you're right. Plunge right into it. Well"—he cleared his throat and took another crack at the drink—"I imagine you've heard of John Randolph?"

"The name does seem to be familiar," I said dryly. "What does he have to do with it?"

"Everything. He was the insured. We issued two policies on him. One, straight life. The other, accidental death with double indemnity. As I have said, both will be paid without question. Both, I might add, were for large amounts."

He finished his drink and went into another reverie. I emptied my glass while I waited. Finally I cleared my throat to get his attention.

"I don't quite see," I said, "where I come into the picture. What do you want me to do?"

"A very good question," he said, nodding. Then he did something I never expected to see. He ordered a third round of drinks and waited until they were served.

"John Randolph," he said solemnly, "was a great American. He served almost twelve years in Congress with honor. He was also a friend of several of our directors. I like to think that he was my friend, too. We played handball here several times and then had lunch afterwards."

"Martin," I said gently when he didn't continue, "remember me? March. Milo March. I am what we laughingly call an insurance investigator. I get three hundred dollars a day and expenses. Now, what in hell am I doing here?"

He brought his gaze back to me. "Milo, my boy, you are going to perform a public service."

"Me?" I said in some surprise. I shrugged. "As long as I get the three bills a day and expenses, I'll even go stand on my head in Times Square. What, may I ask, does my new image involve?"

"We had a long board meeting yesterday. We have been distressed by the meaningless killing of Congressman Randolph. We are distressed by the fact that the police and the FBI have not captured the killer after four weeks of an intensive nationwide search. We feel that as Americans and the men who guide a large American corporation, we must do something about it. Intercontinental Insurance is concerned every day of the year with life and death. We believe that it is time, in view of our knowledge and experience, for us to make a contribution to the speedy solution of this terrible crime. As a public service, of course." He paused dramatically. "You, Milo, my boy, are going to solve the murder of John Randolph and see to it that the killer is not only identified but brought to justice—whether it's Crown or someone else."

"Me?" I repeated. This time I thought I sounded a little hysterical. "The best detectives of a dozen cities and states have been working on this for four weeks. So have the FBI agents. Probably two million dollars has been spent on just that. Pictures of the accused man have appeared in every newspaper and magazine and rewards have been posted, so you can guess that there are several million amateurs scurrying around. And they are no nearer a solution than they were more than three weeks ago. They haven't even found Eugene Crown. Now you want me to leap on my little bicycle and go out all alone and correct their failures?"

"Precisely," he said. "We have complete confidence in you, my boy. We have come to appreciate that while your methods are usually quite unorthodox, they have produced results. You have an enviable record of success with us. Therefore, we are certain that you—"

"Please," I interrupted, holding up my hand. I was surprised to notice that it was steady. "No speeches about what a sterling fellow I am. It might go to my head. ... Martin, are you quite certain you are aware that this may cost you a lot of money?"

"It's not the time to be considering costs," he said loftily. "But why do you bring it up?"

"Because it's not like one of our usual cases. They are nearly always one of three or four set methods of fraud, so there is something to work on before we even start. And it hasn't been muddled up by dozens of other people working on it. By the very nature of it, this will probably take longer and will undoubtedly involve a lot of traveling. The travel expenses alone could be pretty large."

He waved his hand as though brushing away a fly. "We have talked about it and are in complete agreement that we must do it. We leave everything else up to you. When you need money ask for it, and you will get it."

I whistled softly. "Boy, when you go public service you go all the way, don't you?"

"Of course," he said, sounding for the moment like his old self, "we shall expect the usual accounting when you render your bill."

"Naturally," I said dryly.

"And it may be easier than you think."

"Why? And don't tell me it's because you have complete confidence in me."

"There have been a lot of theories advanced about the killing. I've noticed that quite a number of people agree on one possibility. They do not think that this was just one man suddenly deciding to kill a political figure for some obscure reason. They believe it must have been a conspiracy and Crown was only a tool. Although I can't imagine anyone conspiring against Randy."

"Randy?"

"That's what Randolph's friends called him."

"Oh."

"If it was a conspiracy," he went on, "then it would mean a well-organized, carefully planned act and so somewhat similar to many of the cases you've worked on. Just your kind of case, Milo, old boy."

"Oh, sure."

We ordered lunch. And about time, I thought. Martin Raymond was getting a little smashed on his three cocktails, and I had visions of him staggering into the offices.

He finished the omelet he had ordered and leaned back. "We are taking full-page ads in the leading magazines and newspapers. It will be a memorial to Representative Randolph, and below it we will announce what we are doing."

I looked at him. "With no mention of me, I trust?"

"No mention of you," he said. "The members wanted to include your name as our best investigator. One member even wanted to use a small photograph of you. I explained to them carefully that you wouldn't care much for either gesture." He laughed. "I also told them you'd probably take a full-page ad yourself, stating that you were not working on the case and never would work for us again."

"That's all I would need," I said. "I could start making my own funeral arrangements the next day. Thanks, Martin. I hope you always remember that publicity is the worst present you can give any of your investigators. Especially me. When do you want me to start?"

"Right away. You can bill us starting with today."

I shook my head. "Martin, Martin, you disappoint me. No complaining about my daily charges and an unlimited expense account? You've taken half the fun out of working for you."

He waited until the waiter cleared the table and brought us our coffee. "I'm glad you reminded me," he said with a smile. "If you stop in and see my secretary anytime this afternoon, she will have some expense money for you. I expect we'll hear from you when it's gone."

"I'll probably start by investing in a couple of drinks while I sit and brood somewhere. Hell, I don't even know where to start on a case like this."

"You'll think of something. Why not start here in New York? This Crown was here for a few days, according to the papers."

"Yeah," I muttered.

We talked of other things while we had coffee. He signed the check, and I walked out with him. The food had apparently cleared his head, and he was none the worse for the three cocktails. Maybe I'd underestimated him. He might have gotten drunk on the idea of performing what he considered a "public service." My instinct told me that the cops and the FBI might have a different idea about it.

I let him take the first taxi. I got in the second one and told the driver to take me to the Public Library. He looked at me as if he thought I was out in left field, but he threw the flag and drove off.

I had decided that I wouldn't go to the office for a couple of hours, and I might as well make good use of the time. When I reached the library, I went to the periodicals room and got several issues of the *New York Times,* starting with the morning following the assassination. When I finished the first batch, I went and got another. I read every word faithfully and managed to keep most of the facts in my head.

At three o'clock I decided I'd had enough for one day. I made a note of the last issue I'd read and turned the newspapers in at the desk. I went out the Fifth Avenue door, crossed the street, and walked over 42nd Street to Madison Avenue.

"Milo," I said to myself as I waited for a taxi, "it is my opinion you have just qualified for the services of a head shrinker. You have stuck your neck into the biggest damned noose ever invented."

THREE

The taxi let me out in front of the glass and stone building that was the Intercontinental Building. There were times when I thought it looked like a mausoleum; frequently when I was with Martin Raymond I was certain of it.

There was the usual beautiful receptionist sitting behind the desk when I stepped out of the elevator. I stopped to admire her.

"Yes?" she asked, looking up.

"I'm Milo March," I said. "I sometimes labor in these vineyards. Would you please tell Mr. Raymond's secretary that I'm here requesting permission to land?"

She smiled and nodded. She picked up her phone, pressed a button, and announced my name. She replaced the receiver, and her smile was more personal as she looked at me. "You may go in, Mr. March."

"Thank you," I said. I lingered for a minute. "How long have you been working in this glorified soup kitchen?"

"Three weeks." She laughed softly. "I presume you know your way to the office?"

"I've been crawling to it on my hands and knees for years now. I'll see you on the way back—if I make it through the enemy lines." I turned to the left and went through the door, then down to the corridor to the office. Martin's secretary had a small office directly in front of his.

"Hi, honey," I said, stopping in front of her desk. "I hear that you have something for me."

"Yeah," she said dryly. She picked up a slip of paper and handed it to me. "If you ask me, I think you and Mr. Raymond have blown your cotton-picking minds."

"Why do you say a thing like that?" I glanced at the paper in my hand and then had to take another look because I couldn't believe what I'd seen the first time.

"It's simple, junior. Mr. Raymond spent the entire morning acting like a kid who's going to his first birthday party. When he came back from lunch he did everything but skip down the corridor. At first I thought he was smashed, but then I realized they don't make booze that strong. And you! You've got five great big ones waiting here for you—signed by a man who screams in mortal agony when he has to give you a thousand dollars—and it takes you two hours to get around to picking it up. The whole world has gone nuts."

"Haven't you heard, dear one?" I said. "We're doing a public service."

"Yeah? You working for nothing?"

"You wound me, honey. The public part is free, but for the service part I'm charging my usual fee."

"That's what I thought. Okay, run along with your ill-gotten gains. The cashier will probably be so undone when she sees the paper that she'll have to leave for the rest of the day."

I smiled at her and went on down to the cashier's cage. I handed the slip to the girl. I noticed that she did a double take, too. And she had to clear her throat before she spoke. "How do you want this, Mr. March?"

"In hundreds will be fine," I said as if I did it every day.

She counted out fifty of them, waited until I had signed the slip, and gave them to me. Five thousand dollars. And that was only the advance expense money. I folded it with respect and put it in my pocket.

"Subway fare," I told her. "I'll see you when I get back."

I returned to the reception room and stopped for another look at the girl. "I just tapped the company till," I said. "Why don't I spend some of it on lunch for you?"

"I've already had my lunch," she said.

"Okay, we'll make it dinner tonight."

She laughed. "I'm busy tonight, Mr. March. And you've made me lose a dollar."

"Me? How?"

"I was talking to one of the girls who used to work at this desk, and I told her you had just come in. She bet me a dollar that on the way out you'd ask me to go to lunch and that if I said no you'd try to make it for dinner."

"Sorry about that. I'll tell you what. Let's make it for dinner tomorrow night. The dinner and a few drinks will give you a profit on the dollar. That'll make it a fair game."

She laughed again. "The same girl told me that if I went out with you, I'd be the game."

"That's the trouble with this place," I said darkly. "There's too damn much gossip." I turned and went to the elevator. "You'll regret this fifty years from now." I stepped into the elevator and stood in dignified silence while the doors closed.

Normally at this point, I might well have taken my pocketful of money into the nearest nice bar to spend the rest of the afternoon brooding over the future. Instead, I went back to 42nd Street and browsed in the secondhand magazine stores. I found copies of *Time, Life, Look,* and *Newsweek,* as well as several less well-known magazines, covering the past four weeks. I tucked them under my arm and took a taxi to my apartment on Perry Street in Greenwich Village.

I made a pot of coffee and called my answering service and told them I was on a job and to take all messages until I got back to them. I put a cup of coffee on the end table and settled down to reading the magazines. This time I made notes.

By seven o'clock I still wasn't through with the magazines, but my eyes felt as if they were. I got up, put my jacket on, and went out. I walked down to the Blue Mill on Commerce Street.

I stopped at the bar, said hello to Alcino, the bartender, who was my friend,* and ordered a dry martini. I nursed it along, enjoying every swallow. When it was finished, I ordered another. Then I went back to one of Manny's tables. I ordered a rare steak, potatoes, and a salad.

Afterwards, I went straight back to the apartment and to work. It was fairly late when I finished the magazines. I had marked passages in all of them as I went along. I went over to my desk and started writing out a list of known and unverified reports.

From the record, Eugene Crown had been a born loser. He had started a life of petty crime when he was sixteen. Before the last four weeks, he had never risen above that. His biggest

---

* The Blue Mill was a real place, and Alcino Neves a real person. The author lived on Perry Street in the Village, and the Blue Mill was indeed his favorite bar. (All footnotes were added by the editor.)

take had been three thousand dollars, his smallest ten, and his average between one and two hundred dollars. He had obtained no more than seven thousand dollars from all his crimes and had been able to spend no more than half of that, because he had usually been caught shortly after every crime. The only thing he gained was several years in prison.

He was a born loser in other ways too. Once a cop caught him breaking into a place and he ran. He rounded the corner only to run right into the arms of a second cop. Another time he was caught inside a store by a cop. Crown pulled a gun on the cop, but he'd forgotten to put bullets in the gun. That time he got shot in the shoulder as well as a trip back to prison. Several times he had tried to break out of prison, but each time he was caught almost as soon as he started. On his last arrest he'd drawn a twenty-year sentence, with little hope of a parole, because of his record.

It apparently never occurred to him that he was in the wrong business. But finally, at long last, he was successful. After serving two years on his twenty in the state prison at Columbus, Ohio, he had managed to escape.

Not only that. He had succeeded in vanishing for four weeks. According to everything I'd read, the police had no idea where he had been from the day of his escape until the murder of Congressman Randolph. His fingerprints were found on the murder weapon and, later, on the car he had used. Then the police found out that he had been in a few places during that first four weeks. His photograph had been recognized by people in Cleveland, New York City, Chicago, and Los Angeles. All before the assassination. He'd been driving an almost-new red Mustang then. It had been abandoned in Akron, Ohio, after the shooting in Cleveland.

After that, nothing. It was as if Eugene Crown had been swallowed up by the earth. Maybe, I thought suddenly, he had been.

I looked at my watch and saw that it was later than I thought. Tomorrow would be a busy day. Probably all the days would. I poured myself a big drink of V.O., swallowed it, and went to bed.

It was early in the morning when I awakened. I put on some coffee and began looking at my notes while I had the first cup. Then I made myself some scrambled eggs and toast and continued looking at the notes while I ate. Another cup of coffee and I was ready to start planning the day—or as ready as I'd ever be.

I put in a phone call to Johnny Rockland. Lieutenant John Rockland. He was the head of a special squad of detectives. He was in his office and came on the phone at once.

"Good morning, Milo," he said. "This is a little early for you. What do you want from me this time?"

"Me?" I said, trying to sound surprised. "It's been a long time since I've seen or talked to you, and I thought I'd give you a call."

He laughed. "Whenever you start patting me on the back, I keep looking over my shoulder for the knife. What is it?"

"As a matter of fact, I want to take you to lunch. I do want to talk to you. But not on the phone. It'll take too long."

"You sound serious, Milo."

"I am. Can you make it for lunch?"

"I guess so, if nothing too pressing comes up. Want to meet me here?"

"No. Meet me at Whyte's. At the bar. Twelve-thirty?"

"Okay. If anything comes up, I'll call you. Where are you? At the office?"

"No. At home. I'll see you later, Johnny."

I hung up and left and walked to Sheridan Square to pick up the morning papers. Then, back to the apartment.

I checked through the papers to see if there was anything new. There wasn't, except for a small story on the sixth page of one paper. It said that "according to reliable sources" the FBI now believed that Crown had managed to get out of the United States and were broadening their search to cover other parts of the world. What parts, it didn't say. So I went back to my notes.

They were pretty thoroughly memorized when it was time for me to go. I put on a tie and jacket and went downstairs. I found a taxi at Sheridan Square and told the driver to take me to Whyte's.

It was one of the oldest, and still one of the best, restaurants in New York. It was way downtown, so it wouldn't be too far from where Johnny was based.

We reached the restaurant shortly before twelve-thirty. I paid the driver and went into the bar. Johnny wasn't there, so I ordered a martini and waited. He came just as I finished it.

"Hello, Johnny," I said. "Let's go upstairs. It won't be crowded this time of day."

He nodded, and we went up the stairs and took a table in the corner. The waiter came over.

"Want a drink, Johnny?" I asked.

"What are you doing? Trying to corrupt the Force?"

"Why not?"

"Okay. I'll have a bourbon and water."

I nodded to the waiter and ordered a martini for myself. He left. Johnny and I talked about indifferent things until the drinks were served.

"What's up?" Johnny asked when the waiter was gone. "I've never heard you sound so serious. Are you in trouble?"

"I think so," I said, "but not in the way you probably mean. I imagine you've heard or read about the assassination of the Honorable John Randolph?"

"I've heard of it. I and my boys are the ones who got the tip that Crown had been here, and checked it out. Why?"

"I'm working on it."

"What? How can you be working on it? The only questions are whether Crown's guilty or not and where he is. No matter how much insurance the Congressman had, it'll have to be paid. Won't it?"

I nodded. "Just the same, I'm on the case as of yesterday. For Intercontinental. They carry the insurance and they are not trying to contest the claim."

"I never heard of such nonsense," he said. "What the hell do they expect to get out of putting you on it?"

"You're not using your head, Johnny," I said with a smile. "They're doing it as a public service. They are going to run full-page ads in magazines and newspapers announcing the fact. That alone will build up their image enough to bring in a lot of new policies. If, later, they can brag that their man did what the FBI couldn't do, they'll be flooded with applicants for policies from the insurance company with a heart."

"All right. I can see that. But what the hell are you doing in it?"

"I'm beginning to wonder myself. Yesterday, when they asked me, I thought of the whole thing as a joke. I figured I'd take it on, travel around the country, getting a fee and expense money, and wait until the FBI grabbed him. But I did a little homework yesterday afternoon and last night. Now I'm not so sure. I think maybe I just sat down in a nest of hornets. What do you know about it, Johnny?"

"Only what I read, Milo. Even our end of it here has been pretty well covered, I think. We stumbled on it by accident. After the killing. We were working on another case, and one of my men went to a rooming house on the West Side. While he was talking to the landlady he heard about this other guy who had lived there. On a hunch he went back with a photograph of Crown. The landlady identified him. He had lived there for two weeks. And that was two weeks before the killing. She thought he was a nice quiet boy."

"Did he have any money then?"

"He must have. He only paid fifteen dollars a week for the room. But the day before he left, he bought that red Mustang. Paid three thousand dollars cash. He got two letters while he lived there, the second one the day before he bought the car. The landlady didn't know who they were from."

"What name did he buy the car under? Crown?"

Johnny shook his head. "Shelby Allister. The same name he used at the rooming house. He took a driving test here under that name, giving the rooming house as his address. He passed, and they gave him a temporary license until the other one could be mailed from Albany."

"Did he see or meet anyone here?"

"Not that we know of. He went out every day, according to the landlady. She thought he was looking for a job. He may have spent part of each day in bars, but we didn't find them. Not that we had much time. The Federal men may have found out more, but all we know about what they've done is what we read."

We ordered two more drinks and told the waiter what we wanted for lunch, but not to bring it until we had finished them. After the drinks had been served, I asked, "What do you think about it, Johnny?"

He smiled. "What do you think about it? You're the one working on it."

"All I've done is some reading and made some notes. I notice there are a lot of different opinions about why Randolph was killed. Some think it was because he was for civil rights, some because he was an anti-Communist, some because he was anti-union, and others because he had attacked the Arab states on the floor of the House. The Congressman had something in his little bag for everyone."

"Not only that," Johnny said, "but there's a large group who are convinced that Crown killed the Congressman all by himself for one of those reasons, and an equally large group that believes he was part of a conspiracy. What's your idea, Milo?"

"Where'd he get the three grand for the car?" I asked.

"A good question. I don't know, and I don't think the Feds know either."

"I presume he also bought insurance for the car like any good, law-abiding citizen. And he lived for the four weeks before the killing. Plus four weeks since then, in which he has managed to elude several hundred policemen, not to mention how many amateurs who have seen pictures of him. All of that costs money. Somebody must have given it to him."

"Why?" Johnny wanted to know.

"Look at his record. He was a born loser. In eighteen years of crime I don't think he got more than seven thousand dollars, and he didn't get to spend all of that. He was caught after or during every job. He tried to shoot a cop without putting any bullets in his gun. The only success he had in his life was the last time he tried to break out of jail. And he must have had help after he made it, or they would have caught him within two or three days. He could never do anything right, and now, suddenly, he's a master criminal. I don't believe it."

He nodded. "So you think it was a conspiracy?"

"Yes," I said. "At least there had to be one person who did the planning and furnished the money. Maybe more but at least one. But you haven't told me what you think."

"I think," he said slowly, "that you're right. Which makes me repeat what I asked before. What the hell are you doing in this?"

"If I had known as much as I know now—or think I know now—I don't think I would have taken the job. But I did take it, and I can't back out without throwing away my best and almost only account. It'll probably turn out to be just another case, only more complicated."

"You know what you're going to be running into, don't you?" he asked curiously.

"What do you mean?"

"Well, to begin with, you'll encounter a lot less cooperation and a lot more hostility from law enforcement bodies, including the FBI, than you normally do. None of them are going to like you messing around in this kind of case."

"What else is new?" I asked with a smile. "That's the way they feel in any kind of a case."

"There's another thing," he went on. "If it is a conspiracy, it may not involve just one other man. There may be a lot of other men. And if they find out you're on the case, and they will, and if you do stumble onto something, they're going to try to cut you down."

"That's been known to happen on other cases, too."

"And," he said, sounding almost angry, "what do you think you can find out that the smartest cops in this country can't?"

"I don't know, Johnny. But I work a little differently, as you know, and I just might stumble onto something. I have a few times. I might even find Crown before they do."

"Where are you going to dig?"

"What?"

"I asked you where are you going to dig. If there was a conspiracy and Crown was used as the executioner, I'll bet you a year's pay that he's dead, and was dead within a day or two of the assassination."

"It's a possibility," I admitted. "I thought of it last night. That would be the smart thing for them to do."

"It would also explain why he hasn't been spotted since

that day in Cleveland. His car was found in Akron, but that's not far from Cleveland."

"I'll let you know," I said with a smile.

On that note, we had our lunch and talked about other things.

Later, as we were saying good-bye in front of the restaurant, I thought of something else. "Have you got any pictures of Crown?" I asked him.

"The ones on the flyer the FBI put out. I've got hundreds of them. I'll give you a bunch if you want to come down and pick them up."

"I'll do that. Probably later this afternoon."

"Okay." He put out his hand. "I think you're making a big mistake—but good luck. Take care of yourself."

"Thanks, Johnny."

I took a taxi uptown to the Public Library and went back to work on the *New York Times* again. This time I took notes.

When I'd finished, I went back downtown by taxi and stopped at police headquarters to pick up the pictures of Eugene Crown. From there I went back to my apartment.

I made myself a drink and sat at the kitchen table, going over all my notes again. It seemed to me that I had done about all I could in New York. I felt certain there was little point in going to the rooming house or trying to find any bars he might have gone to. That must have been thoroughly covered without turning up anything very important. I'd just have to start from scratch, and it would waste a lot of time. If there was an answer, I had a feeling it was somewhere else.

The real starting point was obviously Cleveland. But I suddenly decided that I would make a quick stop in Washington before going on. I called the airlines and made a reservation for Washington for the following morning.

I glanced at my watch. There was just about enough time to catch Martin Raymond before he left his office. I dialed the number and asked the operator for him. His secretary, as usual, answered.

"Hi, honey," I said. "This is Milo March. Is the great public servant still there?"

"I think so," she said. "What's wrong? You spent the bundle of money already?"

"Not quite. I have nine or ten dollars left. You know how it is. The high cost of living keeps going up and up."

"They must have raised the price of martinis," she said dryly. "Just a minute."

Then the great man himself came on. "Milo, my boy, you've got something already. I told you we had complete—"

"Martin," I interrupted, "you have to be putting me on. I told you that this will be a long and expensive case."

"You've lost the money," he said accusingly.

I was sorry I'd called him. "No, I haven't lost the money. I just called to tell you I think I've done all I can here and I'm leaving for Washington in the morning. I'll keep in touch."

"We'll be waiting to hear from you." Then his voice took on the tones of an Elder Statesman. "Don't forget, my boy, we're depending on you."

"How can I forget it?" I asked wearily. "You're going to remind me every time I talk to you." I hung up without waiting for an answer. Poor Martin. He was so anxious he wanted the report presented as a serial.

I put my notes and some additional paper and several pencils in my briefcase. I picked up the manila envelope with the pictures in it and took one out. Eugene Crown looked almost like several hundred thousand young men. Except for two things it would have been difficult to pick him out of a crowd—a fairly prominent scar on the right side of his face and ears that flared out from the sides of his heads like wings. I imagined that most people would remember him once they saw him. I added the pictures to the briefcase and went out. I had a brief debate with myself and decided to go to the Blue Mill again.

I took my time over two martinis, then had dinner. Afterwards, I stopped at the bar and had a brandy and talked to Alcino for a while. Then I bought the morning papers and returned to my apartment.

The first thing, I decided, was to pack my luggage so it would be ready in the morning. I got out my clothes and placed them on the couch in the living room. I brought in the bag and opened it.

It had a special false bottom, just large enough to hold a gun and a shoulder holster. It was also difficult to detect or to open unless you knew how.

I got my favorite gun from the desk, put it and a box of shells in the false bottom, then added a shoulder holster. I had a feeling I might need them before this case was over.

It didn't take long to pack the clothes. I read the papers, but there was nothing new on the search for Crown. I turned on the television and watched it while I had a nightcap. Then I went to bed.

FOUR

The morning flight to Washington was almost full. I looked around me and wondered why all those people were going to the capital. I glanced at the sign above the entrance to the cockpit and saw that we had reached an altitude where we could smoke. I unbuckled the strap around my waist and lit a cigarette.

A stewardess came back through the plane asking people if they wanted coffee, tea, or milk. Finally she reached me.

"I'll have a martini," I said before she could announce her wares.

"I beg your pardon, sir," she said, looking as if she thought she hadn't heard correctly.

"A martini. You know, like in dry. I haven't had my morning juice yet."

She stared at me as if her first thought was that I must be either mentally unbalanced or drunk, but she must have had a second thought because she finally shook her head to herself and went back to the front of the plane. She returned with the martini and a disapproving glance. I drank the martini slowly, and when I'd finished it I told her she could bring me black coffee with no sugar.

"Do you always," she asked as she served the coffee, "start the mornings like this?"

"Not always," I admitted, "but occasionally. I'd hate to think that every morning was going to start out exactly the same. There'd be nothing to look forward to."

She finally smiled before going on about her duties. I leaned back against the seat and relaxed. It was a short flight and there was no point in trying to get more sleep, but I might as well rest while I could.

We came down on the Washington field, and I went into the terminal. I wanted to see one man there, and if I was lucky I might be able to catch him in time to have lunch with him. He was a well-known syndicated columnist named Peter Knox, whom I'd met several times. I phoned his office, and he was there. He said he'd meet me at the Epicurean for lunch, reminding me that we'd met there once before.

I checked my luggage, then made a three-o'clock reservation on a plane for Cleveland. That should give me plenty of time. I went out and found a taxi and told the driver to take me to the restaurant.

Pete wasn't there yet. I told them I was having lunch with Peter Knox and we'd like a quiet table in the corner. I was taken to one, and I ordered a martini.

I hadn't quite finished it when Pete came in. He saw me at once and came over. We shook hands and asked each other foolish questions about how things were going, how we felt, and all the polite little things people jabber at each other day after day. Finally, he was seated across from me.

"Well, Milo," he said for the second time since he'd arrived, "it's good to see you. What brings you to the talking capital on the Potomac?"

The waiter arrived with two martinis without being given the order. He didn't know me, but I guessed he knew Pete pretty well. I waited until he was gone.

"I'm actually on my way to Cleveland," I said, "but I thought I'd stop off and see if you could give a personal picture of one of your talkers. I gather he was a champion talker."

"I'll help you all I can, Milo. But here they are all champion talkers. Which one do you have in mind?"

"Representative John Randolph."

He whistled softly, and a look of speculation came into his eyes. "He was certainly a champion among champions. Why him?"

"I'm working on the case."

"You? But why? It's clearly a job for the FBI and the police. Something personal?"

I shook my head. "I was hired day before yesterday by Intercontinental Insurance. They had the gentleman insured."

"But they certainly can't get out of paying off, can they?"

"They're not even trying to. They're doing what they call a public service. Building a new image. The insurance company that cares. The insurance company with a heart."

He leaned back and laughed until the tears were rolling down his face. "Now I've heard everything," he finally gasped. "But what the hell are you doing mixed up in a stunt like that?"

"Baby," I said, "for three hundred dollars a day and expenses, I'll go out and find out who killed Cock Robin. I'll even let them photograph me putting the arm on the Sparrow—wasn't that who knocked him off?—if they don't show my face in the photograph."

He was still laughing. "That's great. Do you mind if I use it in my column?"

"They'd love it. In fact they're going to run full-page ads in newspapers and magazines, pointing out, in small type but not too small, what they're doing. They'll probably be out in a few days, so you can get the jump on them. But don't mention my name."

"Why not?"

"Don't be foolish," I said. "I don't need any publicity on any case—especially this one. You want me to get shot, boy?"

"Okay, no mention of you," he said. "What do you want to know about Randy?"

"Just a picture of him."

"It'll be hard to keep in focus. In a way, Randy was the perfect politician. He was all things to all men. He probably kept a file on various political groups all over the country and could tell by who was sponsoring his talk what kind of talk to give. If he did make a mistake and pulled out the wrong speech, he'd go ahead and give it with a twinkle in his eyes that made them believe that he was doing this because he had to in order to get votes from those other people, but that he was really with them. Quite a boy was Randy, and he could have gone on being reelected until he was a hundred and ten—if he'd lived that long."

"Ambitious?" I asked.

"I don't think so," he said. "I think he enjoyed being in the House and, I'm sure, felt safer there. If he had started getting bigger, he probably wouldn't have been able to ride so many horses at the same time."

"How'd he get away with it?"

Pete motioned to the waiter to bring us two more drinks. "Randy was clever. He'd make a great speech in support of civil rights, and all the rednecks and the far right would hate him. Then he'd make an anti-Communist speech suggesting that they were really responsible for the race riots, and the far right would think they must have misunderstood his position. He handled everything that way. He introduced a lot of bills in the House that he knew would never get anywhere, but he'd mail copies of the bill to those he knew would like it. He once wrote a bill to have all the Communists in this country stripped of citizenship and sent to Russia by something he called Free America Airlift. Some people thought it was the greatest thing since the Magna Carta. Others never saw it."

"He made a lot of speeches all over the country, didn't he?"

"You can bet he did. Politicians of all stripes and all states loved to have him. He'd make the kind of speech they wanted, and he'd see that copies of them were sent to people who would be pleased. You know, I can't help feeling sorry for that man he was speaking for in Ohio. Poor fellow never got to make his speech."

"He'll probably be elected in a landslide," I said. "All he has to say is something about the Honorable Randolph laying down his life to get him into the Senate."

He laughed. "I expect you're right. You know that Washington is a cruel town. There were always jokes about how many speeches he made, and the day after he was killed, one of his colleagues was going around the Hill saying that as usual Randy had gotten the last word."

"How did the newspapers handle him?"

"Gently. I think he amused most working newspapermen. Of course, he never got much national coverage except when it was a dull day in politics, and then they'd go easy on him."

"I suppose he made a lot of friends," I said thoughtfully, "but didn't he also make a lot of enemies?"

"Most politicians make their share of both. Randy just worked a little harder at it and maybe made more of both."

"Pete," I said, "who do you think killed him?"

"That's a tough one," he answered. "Oh, I suppose the trigger was pulled by that idiot they're looking for now. But he must have had some help. With money, if nothing else. That help could have come from any one of several widely separated groups. It might have come from Communists, Fascists, even the Arabs: Randy usually took the side of Israel, especially in large cities. And he offended many smaller groups. It might have even been a single, solitary crackpot."

The waiter came over and we ordered lunch.

"You know," Pete said then, "if there was a conspiracy, as a lot of people think, then Crown must be either dead or out of the country. And his fellow conspirators are liable to be very interested in anyone who's trying to find him. Especially someone like you. They could knock you off without too much of a fuss being made."

"Yeah," I said. "I thought about it. But I also could have stayed home and had a fatal accident in the bathtub. And if something does happen to me, maybe Intercontinental will run another public service ad."

He laughed again. "The insurance company that cares. I think I'll use that, if you don't mind."

"Be my guest," I said. "Only don't forget, I don't want a byline."

We had lunch and talked of casual things. He filled me in on the latest Washington gossip, including who was fighting with whom and who was sleeping with whom. When we'd finished with lunch, I thanked him for helping me out.

"It was nothing," he said. "You more than repaid me with that line about the insurance company. Good luck, Milo."

We found two taxis, and he went back to work, and so did I, by going to the airport and catching the plane to Cleveland.

This, too, was a short flight, and I relaxed and didn't even think about the case. I needed more information before I could think much beyond the point I had already reached. So I just sat there and half dozed between cigarettes until we came down. I took a taxi to a hotel downtown near the Square and checked in.

It was too late in the day to expect to do any work until the next morning, so I undressed and took a shower. By that time I'd decided I wouldn't go out on the town, so I'd leave shaving until the morning, too. I got dressed in a pair of slacks and shirt and called room service. I asked them to send up all the local newspapers, morning and afternoon, and a bottle of V.O. and a bucket of ice.

It wasn't late enough for the evening news, so I didn't touch the television set. The waiter was there before long. I signed the check and added a tip while he was putting everything down.

When he was gone I poured a drink over ice and stretched out on the bed with the newspapers. At first I skimmed through them to see if there was any mention of Crown or the late Representative Randolph.

There was a small paragraph in the afternoon paper which stated that a recently conducted poll showed that former State Senator Jerry Hayes was heavily favored to win the seat in the United States Senate in the special election which was being held. There was a final sentence noting that the great Representative John Randolph had been brutally assassinated while speaking in behalf of Hayes and that the search for the killer was still continuing.

So much for glory, I thought. Randolph had been temporarily reduced to one sentence on page 7, and a Jerry Hayes was riding to success on the shoulders of a man no longer with us. I turned to other parts of the paper.

When I'd finished, I poured another drink and turned on the television set. As it warmed up, I wondered idly where Eugene Crown was at the moment. It was illogical, but I had a feeling he was still alive. But if he had been used by others, why had he been permitted to live? And how, even with help, had he managed to keep from being caught? For eighteen years he had displayed a genius for being caught. Now, suddenly, he was the Gray Ghost of America, slipping through the fingers of our famous national law enforcement officers and away.

Later, when I felt hungry, I called room service and had some dinner sent up. After coffee, I turned back to the idiot box. I was watching Johnny Carson when I fell asleep.

Hugh Downs and the *Today* show were on when I awakened. I went into the bathroom, splashed cold water in my face, and went back to sit on the bed and light a cigarette. So far, everything was running on automatic pilot. Mornings are always like that for me no matter how much sleep I had the night before.

There were still a few small chunks of ice in the bucket, so I threw them into a glass and splashed V.O. over them. By the time I'd drunk half of it, I was beginning to sit up and take notice. I phoned room service and ordered ham and eggs, toast, and a pot of coffee.

After breakfast and a shave, I went out and made my way to police headquarters. I identified myself and stated what I wanted and was then passed, without much enthusiasm, from cop to cop. I recited the same thing to five of them and finally ended up in the office of a lieutenant who also gave me the fisheye.

"Your name's Milo March?" he asked.

"Yes," I said.

"Insurance investigator? Intercontinental Insurance?"

"Right."

"What do you want?" he asked bluntly.

"I'd like to ask you a few questions about the assassination of Representative Randolph here."

"Why? Everything that's for public consumption has been printed in the newspapers."

"Maybe," I said. "But I thought you might have some facts that weren't published and would be willing to discuss them with me."

"Everything that's proper to release to the public," he said slowly, "has been given to the newspapers. Besides, we don't make a habit of opening our files to just anybody who wants to look at them. Why don't you try the Federal Bureau of Investigation? They're on the case." He gave me a nasty grin.

"Okay," I said. I walked to the door and opened it. I looked back at him. "I thought maybe you were solving it yourself." I closed the door gently.

I had worked in Cleveland on a case a couple of years before, and I had done a favor for a man who was fairly important in the city.* I went to a public phone booth and called him. We cut up old touches for a few minutes and then I told him my problem.

"The man for you to see," he said then, "is Larry Evans. On the *Cleveland Press.* He covered the story, and he's a good friend of mine. I'll call and tell him you're coming over. You can level with him, and he'll level with you. Will you be in town long?"

"That partly depends on your friend," I said. "I'd like to leave today if it's possible. I have a feeling that it's a long road."

"I think I know what you mean. But why are you on it? It doesn't sound like an insurance action."

"The company is in it for glory. I'm in it for bread. And I don't like being told that I'm supposed to go out and beat the FBI and the city cops at their own game."

He laughed. "I seem to remember—at least about the first part. What is it, three hundred a day and expenses?"

"Yes," I said. "Five big ones to start with, more to follow as needed."

* See *Uneasy Lies the Dead* by M.E. Chaber.

"All right," he said. "Have fun. I'd like us to get together, but if you can't, you can't. You see Larry, and the next time you're out in the boondocks, get in touch."

"Will do," I said. "And thanks."

"Not needed. You earned several free rides with me. I'll call Larry as soon as we hang up. I'm sure he'll tell you what he knows. And on one of these trips, set aside one night so we can get together." There was a moment of silence. "Good luck, Milo."

I thanked him and hung up. I walked over to the *Press* building, which was only a few blocks away, and asked for Larry Evans. He came out almost immediately. He was a slim young man who grinned as he came to shake my hand.

"That was fast," he said. "I just hung up from being told that you would be here."

"It's the atomic age," I said gravely. "I know you're busy, and I want to ask you some questions. If you'll be free, suppose we meet for lunch and I can get through it without ruining your work day."

"That sounds good," he said. "I may be busy until noon."

He told me where to meet him for lunch, and I left and went back to the hotel. On the way, I picked up a newspaper, but there wasn't anything in it. At least, not anything I wanted.

At twelve-thirty I went to the restaurant he'd mentioned. He was already there. We went to the table and ordered two drinks.

"It was a dull morning," he said. "What else can I tell you?"

"I don't know," I said honestly. "I was told that you worked on the story about the assassination of John Randolph. I'm interested in it. I've talked—or tried to talk—to one of your local detectives, and all I got was a chill. Chills I can get by staying home and sleeping in the nude in front of an open window."

He smiled. "Who'd you talk to? Lieutenant Whitaker?"

"That sounds like the name."

"He's all right, but he starts off with the idea that amateurs should stay out of cases, and then he's not too happy because the FBI moved in on what he thought was his case." There was an interested look in his eyes. "As I understand it, you are not a police officer. What is your interest in this, and how do you justify trying to be involved in it?"

It was my turn to smile. "Those are good questions. I'll answer them in the order they were asked. I am an insurance investigator. I work for Intercontinental Insurance Company, Incorporated. With cops, my so-called title is a dirty name because they don't think I'm a cop; with others it's a dirty name because they think I am a cop. So the only place I can win is in making a buck. Which I do. So Intercontinental tells me to go find out who killed Randolph and where the killer is at the moment, and I move. Inspired, I grant you, by the noble experience of getting some of that long green. You want to find fault with that?"

"I'll buy it—up to a point," he said. "What are your other reasons for being in it?"

"Off the record?"

He sighed. "If you insist—off the record. But with the understanding that I get a bonus at the end. If that's possible."

"That's fair enough. Now, your first question is really why

is my insurance company interested enough to pay me good money to stick my nose into it. A fair question. They carried insurance on Randolph—which they are paying without question. But they are taking ads in papers and magazines, telling the world what a great man Randolph was and as a public service they will do everything to bring the vile assassin to court and punishment.

"Now," I said, "we come to the second question. What am I doing in it? First, Intercontinental is begging to pay me. Secondly, they are in essence saying that they know that so far a number of police departments and the FBI are falling on their faces, but their man—Milo March—can deliver. I'm an arrogant bastard, so who am I to argue with them? And here I am."

"I'll buy that," he said with a smile. "Actually, everything we know has been published. Crown, so far as we can determine, arrived in Cleveland three days before the assassination. He rented an apartment next to the park where the killing took place. In fact, it overlooked the park. He paid the first and last months' rent and a fifty-dollar cleaning charge. In cash. So far as is known he had no friends here. He did appear in a couple of bars on Euclid Avenue during the three days, but he said nothing that was important. He claimed that he had a job here, to start in three or four weeks, but didn't say where it was. He said he was going fishing for a week or two. This was to the apartment manager. She saw him coming into the building with what could have been a fishing rod. Could have been a gun, too."

I nodded. "And you mean that's all you have?"

"All that has any importance. Lieutenant Whitaker did think he had a hot lead in the beginning, but it didn't hold up."

"What was it?"

"A local, not very important hood named Joe Capo. He has a record but nothing that would tie him in with the case. The only thing that brought him into it at all was that he lives in the same building where Crown rented his apartment. But Capo has lived there for two years, and there was nothing that ever tied the two of them together at any time. So it was dropped by the locals and by the Feds."

I paid for the lunch, thanked him, and promised I'd let him know if I picked up anything. Then I took a taxi to the building where Eugene Crown had rented an apartment. I looked up the manager, a little, slim old biddy who was still enjoying her brief stay in the limelight. Capo had lived there for the two years, was still living there, and she considered him a good tenant. She thought the police were too rough on him and said he'd never been in any trouble while living there and he was a nice man. The only thing she knew about what he did was that he was a "traveling man" and was usually on the road. That's where he was at the moment.

I went back to the hotel and phoned Larry Evans at the paper. He came on right away.

"Milo March again," I said. "I forgot a couple of things I wanted to ask you. How long was it after the assassination that the police located the spot from which the shot was fired?"

"Not long. Only a few minutes after they arrived. Someone

thought they saw the shot fired from a window on the fourth floor of that building. Someone else was found who saw a man run out of the building and drive off in a red car. They found the rifle in the apartment on the fourth floor where Crown was living; then they learned that Crown owned a red car, and, as you know, they later found the car."

"But the witness didn't actually identify Crown as the man seen running from the building?"

"No. But there seems to be no doubt that it was Crown. Incidentally, the apartment was rented and the car was registered in the name of Shelby Allister."

"I knew about that name on the car. Crown rented the apartment himself, didn't he?"

"As a matter of fact, he didn't. Someone, saying he was a friend of Crown, rented the apartment and paid the rent. Crown showed up two days later, got the keys from the manager, and moved in. They never found the man who rented the place. All the manager could remember was that he was, although he was fairly young. I understand that she was shown dozens of pictures of known criminals but was unable to identify anyone. The only other interesting thing she had to say about him was that he especially asked for an apartment facing the park."

"That is interesting," I said. "The description, even though it refers only to his hair, may be misleading. He could have dyed his hair. One more thing. Does the paper have any photographs of this Joe Capo you were telling me about?"

"I think we have a few," he said. "Why? You onto something?"

"Not a thing," I said cheerfully. "I'm just curious. I'm not onto anything. But if I do stumble onto something, I'll let you know. Could I get two or three shots of Capo?"

"Sure. I'll have them ready for you in about an hour."

I thanked him and hung up. Then I called the airport and made a reservation on a flight to Columbus. I packed my things and went down and checked out. I spent my time waiting in the bar.

Later I took a taxi to the *Press* building and had the driver wait while I went upstairs. Evans was out on a story, but he had left a manila envelope for me. I took it and went down to the taxi and told the driver to take me to the airport.

There were a few minutes before flight time. I checked in my luggage, picked up my ticket, and waited in the bar until it was time to board the plane.

It was about half full when we took off a few minutes later. When the stewardess came around, I ordered a dry martini and waited until she had served it. As soon as she was busy with other passengers, I opened the envelope and took out the pictures. There were four of them.

Joe Capo would have been typecast if he'd ever gotten a job in Hollywood. He looked like a dozen other hoods I'd met. There was one full-length picture of him walking out of a building with several other men, and it was obvious that Joe was not very tall. He was well dressed, about forty years old, slightly on the pudgy side, and his complexion was dark. There was a dour expression on his face, but that was probably because he didn't like having his picture taken.

Slipping the photographs back into the envelope, I leaned back in the seat, sipped the martini, and thought.

Nothing much had turned up so far. I had a lot of information, but anybody who could read had as much. The man with the white hair was interesting, but the police had as much as I did, maybe more. That left only Joe Capo.

All I had there was that I didn't like coincidences, so I was beginning to get a driving curiosity about Joe. Maybe the police had lost their curiosity. If so, it might give me a slight advantage. But it was a hell of a thing to build a case on.

FIVE

It was still early in the day when we landed in Columbus, but by the time I reached the hotel I decided it was too late to go to the prison. But there was one other thing I wanted to do and there should be enough time for that. I checked into the hotel, unpacked what I would need, then took a quick shower and changed clothes. I took the phone book and looked up the name Crown.

There were several listed, but there was only one Benjamin Crown. But there was also something called the Crown Pub. I remembered that the stories had mentioned that Eugene Crown's brother ran a bar in Columbus. I made a note of the address, then went downstairs and took a taxi there.

The exterior of the bar was in an early English style and really did look like a pub. When I got inside I saw that the same style was there, too. It was an attractive place.

There were only a few customers, all of them congregated at one end of the bar. I walked to the other end and took a stool. The bartender walked slowly toward me. He was a heavyset man, probably in his middle forties, with thinning brown hair.

I ordered a dry martini and waited until he'd set it before me, taken my money, and returned with my change.

"Is the owner around?" I asked casually.

Something in his face changed. "I'm the owner," he said.

"Are you Eugene Crown's brother?" I asked bluntly.

Then his face changed radically. His lids dropped partly over his eyes, and the only expression on his face was one of weariness. "Yeah, I'm Ben Crown. I'm also, as you probably know, an ex-con. Now, what kind of fuzz are you?"

"Relax," I said with a smile. "Actually I'm not fuzz at all. I work for an insurance company, and they're paying me to see what I can do—which might even include running interference between your brother and the cops. I don't represent any special threat to him, and I certainly don't threaten you in any way. I'd like to talk to you about your brother, but I won't take up too much of your time."

"What's the difference? I've answered the same questions over and over. Now I know them by heart. No, I didn't know Gene was going to try to escape from prison. No, I didn't know he was going to be mixed up in anything. No, I haven't heard from him or seen him since he did escape, and I have no idea where he is now. That sums up my knowledge about it."

"I wasn't going to ask any of those questions, Mr. Crown. The only question I want to ask which might even come close to them is this one: Do you think your brother shot John Randolph?"

A touch of surprise crossed his face. He looked directly at me, instead of through me, as he had been doing. "He might have," he said softly, "but only if he was promised a lot of money."

"What would be a lot of money to him?"

He smiled tightly. "I've seen times when fifty bucks was a

lot of money to Gene. If somebody told him they wanted him to do something like that, his idea of a lot of money might go up to twenty-five grand or so. I don't really know. I haven't seen too much of Gene in years. When he was in the slammer, I used to visit him maybe once a month and see that he had cigarettes. When I used to get in the slammer, he'd visit me once in a while—if he wasn't in, too. That's all."

"You weren't close?"

"That about sums it up. I guess I felt a little guilty, thinking that he started all of this because he wanted to imitate his older brother. Maybe that's why I always tried to visit him."

"Any other brothers and sisters?"

"No. Just Gene and me."

"Where were you raised?"

"About ninety miles from here," he said. "Did you ever hear of Athens, Ohio?"

I nodded. "That's where Ohio University is."

"Well, we didn't live there. Just north of Athens there's a road turning off to the east. It runs past old abandoned mines. That's where a lot of Hocking Valley coal used to come from. And there's a little village there that was built by the coal companies. The houses were rented to the miners. The old man used to be a miner, but by the time I can remember he was doing odd jobs. There wasn't much mining then."

He noticed that my glass was empty and went off to mix a fresh martini. When he brought it, he waved away the money I'd put on the bar. "We didn't have much money," he continued, "but somehow we got through. At least those years. Gene and I didn't do so good when we got older."

"Did you both go to school there?"

"Yeah. At least through the grades. Then we went to high school in Athens. But not very far. I got through two years before I dropped out. I was already in trouble by the time Gene started. He didn't quite get through the second year. He got busted in the middle of it."

"What for?"

"He robbed a store and got ten dollars. They got him before he spent more than two dollars of it. On candy. They sent him to reform school."

"He usually got caught right away, didn't he?"

"Yeah." He grinned. "He wasn't cut out for that kind of work."

"And you?" I asked with a smile.

"I guess I wasn't either. But after my third bust, I quit. I've been clean ever since."

"Tell me something else," I said. "Did Gene have a lot of girlfriends?"

"I don't know about later years. We never talked about that. Not many when he was younger. The girls liked him, though. But we didn't have much in the way of clothes and had no money. I always figured he was going to spend the other eight bucks from that first job on a girl. Just a minute." He hurried off to serve the other customers.

"You said a girl," I said when he came back. "You think there was one particular girl he planned to spend the money on?"

"I remember that's what I thought at the time. There was one girl about his age. Sixteen. Pretty, as I remember. And she liked him. I doubt if he even ever held her hand. But I think he wanted to."

"Do you remember her name?"

He frowned for a minute. "Yeah. It was Rhoda Ames—no, that's wrong. It was Rhoda Bentley, then she married a guy named Ames, and was still living in Athens the last I heard. Somebody told me this when I went back at the time the old man died. Haven't been back since."

"Was Gene there, too?"

"No. He was in the slammer at the time. I visited him after that and told him all about it." He stared off into space. "There was something else I was going to tell you about Gene, but what was it? … Oh, yeah. About girls. Like I said, most girls seemed to like him, but he never believed it. I guess you've seen pictures of him?"

I nodded.

"Well, he was kind of funny-looking when he was a little kid. Mostly because of the way his ears stuck out. The other kids called him Bat Ears, and I guess he began to get the idea that no girl would like him. Then when he was fifteen he got in a fight with some other kid and the kid cut him on the cheek. That's the scar you can see in the picture they put on the Wanted sheet." He paused for a minute. "What did you say your name was?"

"I didn't say. It's Milo March."

"Well, you were right about one thing, Mr. March. A lot of your questions are different than the fuzz have been asking. You've made me remember a lot of stuff I haven't thought about for years. You know, I hope the kid gets some kind of break. I'd hate to see him just shot down. Know what I mean?"

"I know what you mean," I said gently. "Maybe he will. That must have been hunting country around where you were raised. Did you and Gene do a lot of hunting when you were kids?"

He laughed. "Only for bottles we could take to the store and sell. The old man had a broken-down rifle, and he used to go once in a while and bring back a couple of squirrels or rabbits. We weren't allowed to touch it, but I remember one time Gene and I swiped it and went out in the woods. We shot it three or four times, but we couldn't hit anything. Yeah, now I remember. ... Gene shot the gun once and then cried. Said it hurt his ears. So we sneaked the gun back in the house, and the old man never found out."

"Would you say Gene was a good rifle shot?"

"Are you kidding? I'll bet he never touched another rifle—until—" He broke off and looked at me.

"Pretty good shooting for a guy who's never held a rifle since he was a little boy," I said. "Maybe he'll get a break—especially if you're right in thinking he never held a rifle since then. But at best I expect he'd go up for conspiracy. I don't think there's any doubt that he's involved in it in some way. ... Mr. Crown, would you say your brother was smart?"

"Not the way you mean smart. Gene was smart like some animals are. If he was cornered, he'd fight like an animal—but he'd rather run. He could usually smell any kind of a trap, but then he'd probably run blindly right into the trapper who had put it there."

I nodded and reached into my pocket. I brought out the picture of Joe Capo. I held it out so he could see it. "Did you ever see this man before?"

He started to shake his head, then stopped the movement. He reached out and took the photograph and stared at it closely for several seconds.

"Yeah," he said finally. "That was a guy who came in here every day for four or five days, back maybe about two months ago. Then I never saw him again. Never did know his name. He wasn't much for talking. The way he acted, I had a feeling he was an ex-con. I remember I once asked him what he did. He said he was a traveling man." He handed the picture back. "Why?"

I put it in my pocket. "He was around here two months ago. Wasn't that about the time your brother escaped from prison?"

"Yeah," he said. He sounded excited. "You think he's mixed up with Gene some way?"

"I don't know," I said honestly. "I'm just curious about him. Maybe he is, maybe he isn't."

"You know his name?"

"Joe Capo."

He thought for a minute, then shook his head. "Don't ring no bell. But I was sure he was an ex-con."

"He probably is. If not, he should be."

"Maybe," he said, "he and Gene were in the same joint sometime. Did you think of that?"

"I thought of it. But thinking of it doesn't make it so." I finished my drink. "Well, thank you, Mr. Crown."

"Sure, Mr. March. Drop in again."

"I'll probably leave town tomorrow."

"Well, maybe the next time you're in Columbus. I sure

hope you can do something for the kid. Let me know if you have any luck."

I promised him I would and went out to get a taxi. I told the driver to take me to the hotel. It seemed to me that I was collecting more and more people whom I was supposed to let know what happened. If I did come across something, it would take me a month to catch up with phone calls.

And if I wanted to be honest with myself, I didn't really have very much. Sure, I had some information about Eugene Crown that possibly the police didn't have, but it wasn't exactly the stuff that would solve anything. Especially where Crown might have gone. That was, I reminded myself, the first thing on the agenda.

Back at the hotel, I stopped in at the bar and had a couple more martinis while I brooded about the whole thing. Finally I wandered into the hotel restaurant and had some dinner. As I left, I stopped in the lobby to pick up all the newspapers I could find, plus a magazine.

In my room I called room service and told them to send up a bucket of ice. I took off my coat and tie and kicked off my shoes. I lit a cigarette and waited. A boy soon arrived with the ice. I paid him off and soon as he was gone, I took off my slacks and shirt. I poured a stiff drink of V.O. over some ice and put it on the stand next to the bed. Then I stretched out with the newspapers and began to go through them. It didn't take long. There was no mention of Crown or the search for him. For the rest, I just glanced at the headlines, but there wasn't anything especially new.

I carried my drink and briefcase over to the small table. I

added to my notes, then went carefully through all the notes once more before putting them back in the briefcase. I walked across the room, poured another drink, and stretched out on the bed again. I lit another cigarette and glared at it.

I was restless and felt like getting dressed and going out to a bar or a club. But I knew damn well what was wrong and that wouldn't solve it. The trouble was that I was completely involved in the case. I also had quite a bit of information. But I didn't have even one theory, and I found it difficult to work that way. On most of my cases it had been relatively easy to start off with at least two theories, sometimes three. That way I would have some idea of which direction I was going, and I could plow straight ahead. I was, more or less, trying to get on the trail of Crown, but that wasn't enough. That could be fixed, I thought. I put all the bits of information out of my mind for the moment and started at the top.

Somebody had shot and killed John Randolph while he was making a speech in Cleveland, Ohio. At the time he died there was no possible clue pointing to a person or persons who had done the killing. Stop there, I told myself, and come back and pick it up later. Who was John Randolph? A successful and handsome politician. A man with many friends—and many enemies. Influential, too. A man who was all things to all people. He had supported Negroes and civil rights—because it was more of a popular cause than it had ever been before, and he was also careful in what part of the country he spoke of that support. He also preached a kind of Americanism that didn't entirely agree with the civil rights movement. He was against Communism and had advocated exiling all

American Communists to Russia. He was against organized labor—except in certain areas, where he was for responsible organized unions. He was against crime and for motherhood. Except for the last two, he was always careful about the part of the country where he spoke on these matters.

For what reason had Randolph been killed? Of course, it was barely possible that he had been killed for a personal reason. He might have been guilty of playing footsie with some man's wife or daughter. But I doubted these reasons. In such a case, the killing would have been less public and less well planned. Why was he killed?

Was it because he seemed to give strong support to Negroes?

Was it because he was quite often anti-Negro?

Was it because he was anti-Communist?

Was it because he sometimes seemed to give strong support to the reactionaries?

Was it because he was anti-labor? Or sometimes pro-labor?

Was it possibly because someone believed that the killing might arouse a particular group to more insurrection and rioting?

Was it (as an afterthought) for a combination of those reasons?

Yes, there were many reasons which might explain his death, most of them political and social. Now it was time for me to go back for a minute. Shortly after the assassination, the police had found where the shot had come from. It was an apartment rented a few days earlier in the name of Shelby Allister. It was covered with fingerprints. The man who had moved in had been seen by the manager, and she had given a good description of him. After the shooting a man had been seen running from the building and then driving off in a red car. The car was later found in Akron, Ohio. It was registered in New York in the name of Shelby Allister.

The fingerprints were sent to the FBI and were soon identified as those of Eugene Crown, who had escaped from the Ohio State Penitentiary four weeks earlier. The manager of the apartment house identified the photograph of Crown. So did a woman who ran a rooming house in New York City where Crown had stayed briefly. So did the man who had sold him the red Mustang. Eugene Crown was wanted for murder and there was a nationwide, maybe worldwide, hunt on for him.

The assassination of Randolph had posed two questions from the beginning. Was his death the work of a single individual? Or was it the result of a conspiracy in which one man had pulled the trigger while the rest of the conspiracy stood back and watched?

I examined the single-individual idea first. If Eugene Crown had fired the fatal shot entirely on his own, why had he done so? There was no evidence of any connection between the two men. There was no evidence that Eugene Crown had possessed any political theories. I also doubted that he had. As near as I could see, he had been driven merely by the urge to steal as much money as he could and spend as much of it as he could before he was caught. Nothing more or nothing less. If he acted all alone, what would he gain by killing Randolph?. One could say that he was mentally ill and wanted to glory in the publicity of being a big man. But to get the glory, he would have to be caught.

But, I reminded myself, Eugene Crown had always been caught within a matter of hours or days. So how had he managed to elude the best manhunters in the country for this length of time?

There was no suspicion that he had pulled any jobs after escaping from prison. So where did he get his money? He had lived for eight weeks by this time, had bought the red Mustang and paid cash, had traveled all over the country. He must have spent as much money in eight weeks as he'd been able to steal in eighteen years. So where did the money come from?

The answer to that question led right back to the conspiracy theory. Somebody had been paying him to do everything he did. Who? How did they first contact him? Was he supposed to kill Randolph or only set up a trail?

If—that big *if*—he had been used by some group in either of these capacities, why hadn't they killed him when he'd finished playing his part? Or had they? Ben Crown had said his brother was shrewd—not his exact words, but that was what he had meant. He'd also said that his brother could smell a trap. Maybe he had smelled one and gotten away. But how? He wasn't smart.

Already I was feeling better. The watchdogs of the conspiracy might get nervous if the Feds snooped around and got close, but they wouldn't dare do anything about it. They couldn't fight the whole FBI. And if they killed one agent, the others would know that he'd been close to something and they would swarm all over the place. But they wouldn't feel so squeamish about a loner poking his nose in here and there.

"March," I said aloud to myself, "I think we're on home grounds now. It's like all the other cases. We push a little here and a little there, and pretty soon somebody will try to push back and you'll catch him off balance. Now all we have to do is be sure to go in the right direction. And be a little conspicuous about it."

I thrust the whole thing out of my mind and turned on the television set. Then I poured myself another drink by way of celebration. I no longer felt like I was floundering around in a lake of Jell-O.

I was up early the next morning. I showered and shaved and got dressed. Then I called room service and ordered a big breakfast, and because I felt so good I ordered a big martini to go with it. I also told them to send up the morning papers. The waiter wasn't long in arriving. He wheeled in the table, poured the martini, and handed me the papers. I paid the check and gave him a big tip. After all, it was only money. And not even mine.

I looked through the papers while I was having the martini. There was one item in a column and that was all. It said that there were rumors that the FBI had found a witness who had seen Eugene Crown boarding a plane for Spain, but that the FBI was refusing to affirm or deny the story.

I ate my breakfast with a good appetite. I packed my things, left them in the room, and went downstairs. I found a classified phone book and looked up car rentals. I went out and took a taxi to the place. After showing all my identity cards and credit cards and signing all the necessary papers, I drove away in a white Eldorado. That, I thought, ought to be conspicuous enough.

Back at the hotel, I had my luggage brought down and signed out. They gave me directions on how to get to the prison.

I found it without too much trouble. I parked the car and went to the gate. I told the guard who I was and that I wanted to see the prison psychologist about a former prisoner. He phoned and then told another guard to take me to Dr. Blake's office. I followed him through several locked gates and doors and wound up in the office.

The doctor was a man of about forty or forty-five. He had a pleasant face with keen eyes behind his glasses. "Your name is March?" he asked.

"Yes."

"And you represent what insurance company?"

"Intercontinental."

"In what capacity?"

"Claims investigator."

"Do you have any identification?"

I pulled the various cards out and put them in front of him. He glanced at them quickly and gave them back.

"Sit down, Mr. March." He smiled. "You'll have to pardon me if I seem a bit surprised, but we don't get many insurance people here—except the ones who stay with us for a time. What can I do for you?"

"I'd like to ask you one or two questions about a former inmate here."

"I'll answer anything I can—and think proper. What's his name?"

It was my turn to smile. "He's rather famous at the moment. His name is Eugene Crown."

"Oh. He is, isn't he? What did you want to know?"

"I'd like your general impression of him—in terms of your profession."

"Well, I see nothing wrong with that. I won't have to look up the file. I did that when the news broke. You understand that he had no kind of therapy here, but I did have several talks with him. He came from a deprived family There was one older male sibling. The mother was in poor health, and the father never had any steady employment that he could remember. He had a great deal of self-rejection and a strong guilt complex, which I think must have gone back to child-hood. With it, of course, went a compulsion to be punished. Do you know anything about his record?"

"Most of it."

"Then you must know that he committed a series of petty crimes, beginning when he was sixteen. He was always caught shortly after the commission of the crime, indicating he unconsciously wanted to be caught. The minute he was punished—that is, imprisoned—he would try to break out, thereby bringing upon himself more punishment. This was so strong in him that I must confess I'm surprised he hasn't been captured before this."

"What would you say he wanted most out of life?"

He smiled. "Consciously? He wanted to get out of prison, have a lot of girls, and improve himself so he would get acceptance and admiration—which he didn't think he deserved. Unconsciously he wanted to be rejected, ignored, and punished, which did fit his image of himself as an unat-tractive bad boy. Have you seen photographs of him?"

I nodded.

"He was very self-conscious about the scar on his face and his rather prominent ears. He was always rubbing at them as if to tear them off his head."

"Would you say he was hostile?"

"I'm quite sure there was considerable hostility in him, but he had long ago learned to turn it against himself. Many persons do this."

"How intelligent was he?"

"Average, but he had never learned to use what he had. It's strange that you should ask that. About a week before he escaped from here, he asked to see me. He wanted to ask me the same question you just asked—about himself."

"What did you tell him?"

"The same thing I just told you. He'd been reading a lot of self-help books, some of them with a little psychology in them. But most of them are sheer pap. Still, he must have gotten something out of them. He seemed more confident that morning. Then he told me that he had decided there were two things he had to do. One was to have his face fixed, and the other was to stop letting people use him. Actually, he said 'making a sucker' out of him. I wanted to get him to talk some more, but at that point he thanked me, knocked on the door, and the guard took him back to his work assignment. That was the last time I saw him."

"Doctor," I said, "do you think he was the sort of person who could have pulled the trigger of that rifle four weeks ago?"

"Any of us could do something like that under the proper

stress. But I will admit that I was somewhat surprised when I learned what had happened."

"Well," I said, standing up, "thank you, Doctor. You've been very helpful."

"I don't see how, but you are welcome, Mr. March. I don't suppose now that I'll ever learn what Crown had discovered about himself."

"If I ever find out, I'll let you know," I told him. I left and followed the guard back to the front gate. I thanked both the guards and went on to the Eldorado.

It was about ten o'clock in the morning. I thought that Ben Crown probably worked the day shift in his bar and then had someone take the night shift, so I should be able to catch him. I found the bar and parked in front of it and went in.

There was nobody there except him, standing behind the bar and polishing some glasses. He looked up as I entered. "Well, good morning, Mr. March. Think of something else?"

"No," I said. "I'm just leaving town, and I thought I'd stop in and have a drink with you before I left."

"Fine. I just opened up, and you're my first customer. What'll it be? The same thing?"

"No. I think I'll have some gin with a little grapefruit in it. In a rock glass, please." I threw a bill on the bar. "Have one yourself."

He mixed my drink and set it down. "It's a little early in the morning for me—but, well, I'll have one with you." He poured himself a straight shot of whiskey. He raised the glass to me and drank. Then he rang up the sale and gave me my change.

"You know," I said, "I've been thinking. There's a lot of talk about your brother going to Europe. Wouldn't it be smarter, since he's on the run, to go to some small town way out in the boondocks, maybe get a job washing dishes and just lay low?"

He shook his head. "That's the trouble with being an ex-con on the run. You've got to have a phony name and a Social Security card to go with it. Other ID, too. That means you can't stay any one place too long. So you can't work long enough to build up a stake, and sooner or later you have to pull another job. And pretty soon you get caught anyway. There's been a lot of cons who broke out and intended to go straight, but then they have to keep moving and getting new cards each time, which ain't easy. The smartest thing to do for him would be to get good forged cards and leave the country. But I don't think he'd know where to get them. I never did."

"I never thought of it that way," I said, which was the truth. The one time I'd needed a forged passport, I'd had no trouble, but I suddenly realized that it had been that I knew the right person to go to for advice. "Well, it wasn't much of an idea anyway. If it had been right, I wouldn't know where to start looking. I'd better get going. Thanks again."

"Thank you, Mr. March," he said. "Stop in anytime."

I went out and got into the Eldorado. I drove until I found Route 33, then headed south. As soon as I reached the city limits, I stepped on the gas and the Eldorado leaped like a spurred horse.

I must have covered about thirty miles when I became consciously aware that there was a black car behind me which had been there ever since leaving Columbus. In the same position, neither gaining nor dropping back. I had noticed it before but hadn't really paid any attention.

When I reached a gas station, I slowed down and turned in. I turned my head to watch the road. The black car swept on by without slowing up. There wasn't much else the driver could do without giving himself away. I got a look at him, but he wasn't anyone I knew.

I didn't need gas, the oil was fine, and so was the water. I thanked the attendant and went back to the highway. I made a little bet with myself. I won it. The next gas station was about five miles down the road. The black car was there. I watched the rearview mirror, and it soon pulled out and followed.

I felt good. It meant that I was going in the right direction and that somebody was interested.

SIX

Driving time to Athens was less than two hours without pushing. I entered a small, pleasant-looking city. I followed the signs and ended up on the main street. I passed the first parking place and took the second. I thought it was pretty nice of me to leave space for him.

I got out and stretched, then locked the car and started walking back the way I had come. I had noticed a small bar around the corner. That's where I was heading, and I was hoping he'd follow me inside so I could get a good look at him. I went past his car without even glancing at it.

The bar was just what I had hoped it would be, a typical small neighborhood meeting place. There were two men drinking beer at the far end, and that was all. I took a stool near the middle of the bar where the mirror gave me a view of the door. I noticed there was a public phone on the wall near the door.

"Yes, sir?" the bartender said, coming up to me.

"A shot of whiskey and a beer chaser," I told him.

I lit a cigarette and waited. The bartender brought a shot glass and a bottle and poured the whiskey. Like most neighborhood bars, he served a generous drink. He carried the bottle back and put it on the shelf, then went to draw the beer. I put a bill on the bar.

Then he came in. I recognized the face from the two glimpses I'd had. He hesitated a moment, then took a stool at the end of the bar to my left. I didn't look at him, but I had gotten a pretty good look in the mirror. He was about thirty-five, not very tall but husky. His black hair was carefully combed. I hadn't been able to see, but I'd have bet that his nails had been recently manicured. His face was a dark olive, and although he was obviously clean-shaven, you could still see his beard. He was well dressed, but there was something just slightly out of focus about his clothes. A perfect picture of a hood masquerading as a reliable member of society.

The bartender brought my beer chaser and went on to wait on the newcomer. He ordered a bottle of beer. The bartender served him, took his money, and gave him change. Then he picked up my money, rang it up, and put my change down in front of me.

"Nice little town you have here," I said.

"We like it," he said seriously. "Your first time here?"

"Yes. I'm on my way through, but thought I'd stop here and have some lunch before going on. Where would you suggest I have it?"

He studied me as if trying to estimate how much I would want to spend. "Well, there are several nice places, but I guess the best in the main part of town is the hotel. It's right around the corner and across the street."

"Thank you. Do you have a public phone?"

"Right over there." He nodded in the direction of the door.

"I wonder if I could trouble you for one more thing? I have to make two long-distance calls. Would you have about five dollars in change?"

"I reckon so," he said, and waited. I pulled out five dollars and put it on the bar. He scooped it up and went to the cash register. I finished my drink while he was gone. I knew that the man on my left had heard all of it, but I was going to give him more for his eager ears.

The bartender came back with the change and dumped it in front of me.

"Thanks," I said. "You might as well give me another one while I'm phoning." I put a dollar down and grabbed a handful of silver.

On my way to the phone I glanced at the man as I would toward any stranger. To ignore his existence would have been a tip-off. He made the mistake of not looking at me.

I dialed the operator and told her I wanted to speak to the air terminal in Cincinnati. She put through the call and told me how much to deposit for the first three minutes. I listened to the musical chimes of the coins, counting them off as I dropped them. When I reached the right number, I stopped, and seconds later I was connected.

"Hello," I said. "I want to make a first-class reservation on a flight to Los Angeles, anytime after six o'clock tonight."

"Just a minute, sir. ... I can put you on a flight at six-thirty."

"Six-thirty is fine. The name is March. Milo March. May I pick the ticket up at the desk?"

"We'll hold it for you until six o'clock."

"That's all right. I should be there by five at the latest. Thank you."

I hung up and waited for the operator to drop the money. The man next to me was pretending complete interest in his beer, but I could almost see his ears twitching. This time, when I got the operator, I asked her to connect me with the Continental Hotel in Los Angeles. I waited while the wires hummed and the operator talked to Los Angeles Information. Finally there was an answer from the hotel, and she told them to wait and once more gave me instructions on the amount to deposit. When it all had chimed its way into the box, she told me to go ahead.

"Hello," I said. "Reservation desk, please."

A moment later another voice came on. "Reservation desk. May I help you?"

"Yes," I said. "I'd like to make a reservation. I'm taking a plane from Cincinnati, Ohio, at six-thirty tonight, their time. I neglected to find out what time it arrives, but I imagine you'll have a schedule, and I'll be on the plane when it arrives. My name is March. Milo March. I've stayed with you several times before."

"Yes, Mr. March. Any particular sort of accommodations?"

"Anything you have—from a broom closet to a suite. Can you confirm a reservation now?"

"Yes, Mr. March. We hope you have a nice flight."

"Thank you," I said, and hung up. Clutching the rest of my change, I returned to the fresh drink that was waiting for me. I put the change down on the bar next to the rest of my change.

"Get through all right?" the bartender asked.

"Yes, thank you. I have my plane reservation from Cincinnati and a hotel reservation in Los Angeles."

"Yeah? Where you from?"

"New York."

"New York?" He grinned. "Sure took a roundabout way to go from New York to Los Angeles, didn't you?"

I smiled. "I guess so, but I had some business to attend to along the way. Besides, it's a nice part of the country to drive through."

"I reckon so. What line are you in, if you don't mind me asking?"

"I don't mind. I think you might call me a research executive. How about another drink while you're on your feet?"

"Sure thing."

While he was getting my drink, the man got up and walked out. As soon as he was gone, I glanced over at his bottle of beer. It was still half full.

"Looks like you lost a customer," I said to the bartender when he returned with my drink.

"Yeah. Makes no mind. Don't care much for strangers who ain't friendly. Now, you—you're the friendly kind."

"I try to be," I said gravely. "Thank you."

I took a dime from the change and went back to the phone. There was a directory hanging from it. I picked it up and looked for people named Ames. There were quite a few of them. I didn't know what her husband's name was, so I decided to start at the top. Maybe I'd be lucky. I put in a dime and dialed the number next to the name of John Ames.

"Hello." It was a woman's voice, so I was one up. "Mrs. Rhoda Ames?" I asked.

"Yes. Who is this?"

"You don't know me, Mrs. Ames, but my name is Milo March. I am just passing through Athens, and I was hoping

I could see you briefly about someone you knew a long time ago. Eugene Crown."

I could barely hear the small gasp on the other end of the phone. "Who did you say you were?"

"Milo March. I'm with an insurance company in New York. Intercontinental."

"I think I've heard of them. I believe my husband has a policy with them. How did you get my name, Mr. March?"

"Ben Crown, Eugene's brother."

"Oh, yes. When did you want to see me?"

"As soon as possible. I'm catching a plane in Cincinnati at six-thirty. I can either come there, or if you'd prefer, I'd be glad to take you to lunch."

"Here would be better, I think. The children will be home in an hour or so."

"I won't take that long. I'll be right there." When I'd hung up, I looked in the phone book again. She lived on North Court Street. I memorized the address and went back to my drink. I downed it.

"Another one, sir?" the bartender asked.

"Not just now. I have to see someone, and then I'll be back."

"Oh, you know folks in town?"

"Not exactly. It's friends of a friend of mine, and I promised to look them up when I came through here." I looked at the bar. There was still almost two dollars in change there. "While I'm gone, buy yourself and those two gentlemen a drink. See you later."

I left and walked quickly down to the corner. There I stopped and looked up the street. The black car was no longer parked where it had been. I smiled to myself. I could guess what he was doing. He wanted to call a report to someone and wanted to be sure of privacy. He had probably gone looking for the local phone company and would make the call from there.

I stopped the first person I saw on the street and asked how to reach North Court Street. When I had the directions, I got into the Eldorado and drove off.

It took no more than ten minutes to reach the house. I parked in front of it and went up and knocked on the door. It was opened by a very pretty young woman with red hair. I knew she was about thirty-four, but she didn't look it.

"Mr. March?" she asked.

"Yes. It's very nice of you to agree to see me."

"I guess I had to, didn't I?" she said with a laugh. "Come in."

I followed her into a small but attractive living room. She indicated the couch, and I sat down. I noticed there was an ashtray on the coffee table in front of me.

"May I smoke?" I asked.

"Of course. I quit a few years ago, but it doesn't bother me." She took a deep breath. "First, I feel I should explain something, Mr. March. When this dreadful thing happened, my husband and I discussed the fact that I had known Eugene and whether I should get in touch with the authorities or not. But we finally concluded that there was nothing I could contribute that they would either want or need. They would have been annoyed that I bothered them."

"That's right. It's been eighteen years since you've seen him or talked to him."

She flushed. "That's not exactly true, Mr. March. That last part, I mean. I've talked to him once. He phoned me the day—it happened."

"That's strange. Where'd he phone from?"

"I don't know. It didn't come through the operator, so he must have dialed directly. He didn't say where he was. All he said was that he'd never forgotten me and that he hoped I was happy. Then he added that I'd probably be reading about him and not to think too harshly of him. Then he said good-bye and hung up. … That wouldn't have helped the police, would it?"

"No," I said, but I wasn't being entirely truthful. They would have probably made the same guess I was making—that the call hadn't gone through the operator because it had been made from Athens or near it. The fact that I was being followed made me sure that he had come this way.

"That makes me feel better," she said. "Now, what did you want to know?"

"Just tell me about him."

"Well, I knew Eugene because we were in most of the same classes at high school. I guess I did like him, but it was not a teenage romance or anything like that. I think I felt sorry for him more than anything else."

"I'll bet you brought home all the stray dogs and cats when you were small," I remarked.

She giggled. "I did, and my mother was always furious. But I didn't take Eugene home. I did feel sorry for him. His family was very poor, and he always wore hand-me-downs. Then he had those funny ears, and to top it off he was always shy.

Almost everyone in school made fun of him, and he didn't know what to do about it. Years later I saw a picture that reminded me of him. It was of a bull in the ring in Spain with all those darts sticking out of his back. He was just standing there with an expression of baffled futility. That was Eugene. I tried to protect him as much as I could. I guess he did think of me as his girlfriend. I wasn't that, but I was his friend— probably the only one he had."

She stopped and thought for a minute. "You know, sometimes now that all of those policemen are looking for him, I can shut my eyes and see him somewhere with that bull's expression on his face."

"Did you think he was intelligent?"

"As intelligent as most of them in the class. At first he had good grades, but the more they made fun of him, the more his grades dropped."

"What did he talk to you about?"

"Mostly about all the big things he was going to do when he grew up, how he'd show them. I think that's what he was trying to do when he robbed that store." She shuddered. "I guess he's shown them this time."

"I think so," I said. I stood up. "Well, thank you, Mrs. Ames."

"Is that all?" she asked in surprise. "I expect it's all I can really tell you, but I thought you'd have dozens and dozens of questions."

I smiled. "No. I'm just trying to build up a picture of Eugene for myself so I'll be able to come close to the way he thinks and the way he'll act. I had to come near here, and I thought

I would stop and listen to what you had to say. I'm grateful to you."

"But why?" She sounded bewildered. "I just can't imagine what an insurance company is doing trying to find Eugene."

"I'm not sure that I know or that they do. Who knows what a corporation thinks? But I'm their chief investigator, and they're paying me to find out exactly what happened and where Eugene Crown is now. I didn't think much about it at the time, but I'm beginning to get a little involved. I don't think that it's as cut-and-dried as saying that on such a date Eugene Crown pulled a trigger and a congressman died. I do think that Eugene Crown has already been tried and convicted, and that if they find him, no one is going to look for much more."

I smiled down at her. "In the meantime, I've gotten curious myself. I'd like to know exactly what happened and why. I'd like to know where Eugene Crown is and get to him before the police do. Maybe I can satisfy my curiosity—and get paid for it at the same time."

"I wish you luck," she said seriously. She opened the door for me. "Oh, what a pretty car. That'll give the neighbors something to talk about." She giggled.

"May I suggest that you tell all of them that I stopped by to look over your husband's policy with Intercontinental."

She stared up at me. "Do you mean my husband, too?"

"I can't give you advice about that," I said with a smile. "Good-bye, Mrs. Ames."

I got into the car, made a U-turn, and went back. On the way, I was thinking about the man in the black car. If my guess had been correct, he had gone to make a report by phone on what he had overheard. As a result, he might have been told to stop following me. Or he might not. I didn't mind if they knew where I was going to be, but it annoyed me to be followed.

So I didn't turn down to the main street but continued parallel with it until I hit Route 50, which was what I wanted. I picked up speed. I stopped briefly in Chillicothe for a sandwich and a glass of milk, then continued on. I reached the Cincinnati airport a few minutes after five o'clock.

I picked up my ticket and paid for it and checked my luggage. I went to a phone booth and called the place in Cincinnati which was supposed to pick up the Eldorado. I told them where it was and that I would leave the keys at the airlines desk. I got some more change and phoned a rental agency in Los Angeles with which I had always done business when I was there. I told them that I was arriving in Los Angeles that night and asked if they'd deliver a white Eldorado to me at the Continental Hotel. They told me they'd do better than that. If I'd give them the name of the airlines and the flight number, they'd have the car waiting for me at the air terminal. One of their employees would be waiting for me at the airlines counter with the keys and the papers I had to sign.

I thanked them and hung up. Then I went into the bar. It was crowded, so I took one of the tables. I knew dinner would be served shortly after we were airborne, so I ordered a dry martini.

I was about halfway through it when the loudspeaker on the wall squawked into life. "Call for Mr. Milo March. Will you please take the call at the ticket counter." I sighed and put down my glass. I told the waitress I'd be right back and went out to the counter. I saw that one of the phones was off its hook. I walked up to the counter and told the girl who I was. She nodded toward the phone. I picked it up.

"Hello," I said. "This is Milo March."

There was a moment of nothing but the hum of an open wire, then the faint click as the phone on the other end was hung up.

SEVEN

That, I thought, was funny. The man in the black car must have made his report and then gone back to check on me. He couldn't find me, and so he must have made a second call to report that. So now someone had called the Cincinnati airport and had me paged to see if the information that had been overheard was correct.

Or maybe they did it for another reason. Maybe they thought it would scare me. It did. It shook me up so badly I had to order a second martini. I had just finished it when the loudspeaker announced that Flight 37 for Los Angeles was now boarding. That was mine, so I got up and joined the others. As we shuffled through the gate, I thought of Eugene Crown doing the same thing to reach a plane that would carry him to safety and wondering if he'd make it.

I found my seat in the plane and sat down. It was a window seat. Not that I cared. I never could figure out why people were so anxious to get window seats. Once you were up in the air, there was nothing to see.

Slowly everyone made it and found their seats, and the door slammed shut. I looked around. It was a full load except for two empty seats. One of them was next to me. I was glad for that because I didn't feel like talking. I reached down and fastened my seat belt.

The sign went on, telling everyone to fasten their seat belts and not to smoke. A moment later we were trundling away from the terminal. I sat and waited patiently, paying no attention to what the plane was doing. The sign would tell me when we were up in the air.

Finally the sign went off and I lit a cigarette. Then I unfastened the seat belt. The stewardesses were already coming down the aisle. One of them came to me.

"We'll be serving dinner soon," she said. "Would you like a drink first?"

"A martini, please."

She moved on. I suddenly realized I was very tired. I hadn't done much, but I felt as if I had worked a double shift in the coal mines and then forgotten to go to sleep. I guess it was more emotional tiredness than anything else.

The stewardess came with the martini. "Tonight," she said, "you have a choice of lobster Newberg or steak, with—"

"If you don't mind, honey," I interrupted, "I'll settle for one more martini and no dinner."

She looked at me, trying to decide if I was drunk or not. I shook my head. "No, honey, I'm not drunk. I'm just very tired. Let me have one more martini and a pillow and I'll sleep all the way to Los Angeles. I can always eat when I get there."

Suddenly she smiled. "All right, sir. I'll bring them to you as soon as I get the other orders."

I leaned back and sipped my drink, occasionally glancing out the window at a wisp of cloud just to be sure we were moving. I had just finished the martini when the stewardess showed up with another one and a pillow.

"Thanks, honey," I said. "I'll remember you in my will. But don't wake me up short of a major crash. After it's over."

She smiled and left. I settled back and worked on the drink. I finished this one faster than the first. Then I tucked the pillow behind my head, put out my cigarette, and closed my eyes. The last thing I remember was wondering who would be my welcoming committee in L.A.

The plane was already on the ground when I awakened. I looked out the window but didn't recognize anything, so I glanced at my watch. I hadn't turned it back yet, but the time indicated this should be Los Angeles. It was. I got up and followed the others out.

I stopped first at the airline counter. I gave my name and wanted to know if anyone had asked for me. He had and he was there. I signed the papers he had with him, and he gave me the keys. Then I went to get my luggage. I was hungry but decided I'd wait until I got to the hotel.

It was a short drive on the freeway, then a few blocks up Sunset and I was there. I told the parking driver I would be going out again soon, tipped the doorman, and followed the boy with my bags in to the desk. I registered and then followed him up to my room.

Room! Hah! They had taken me at my word. It was a suite. Well, I thought, Intercontinental shouldn't mind too much. After all, it was for public service. I shaved, took a quick shower, and changed clothes. I left a suit and laundry on the couch and called valet service to pick them up and have them back to me the next day. Then I went down to the restaurant just off the lobby and had a martini, rare steak, and salad.

After brandy and coffee and a cigarette, I started driving down to Hollywood.

I hadn't thought about being followed when I left the airport, but I was about halfway to Hollywood when I became aware that there was one pair of headlights sticking pretty close to me. I made a couple of moves to test it, and the car stuck right with me. So I had company.

I drove down Hollywood Boulevard until just below Wilton where there's a little bar called Casa Del Monte. It's owned by a guy I know named Leonard Del Monte, but everyone calls him Bo. I parked across the street from it and crossed over without trying to pay attention to the car that had been following. I went inside. There were eight or nine customers at the bar, but the end near the doorway was empty. Bo looked up, surprise on his face.

"Make me a gin and grapefruit juice in a rock glass," I said before he could open his mouth, "and put it up there at the end. I'll be right back." I went on to the rear of the bar and out the back door. That took me to a side street off Hollywood Boulevard. I walked down it, keeping in the shadow of the building.

There was another car about thirty feet behind mine with a man sitting back of the wheel. I couldn't see his face, but I could see enough. He had close-cropped white hair.

So now I knew three of them, I thought as I turned around and entered the bar through the back door. I was still certain that Capo was part of it. I could see Bo making my drink as I walked up the length of the bar. He was someone I would have stopped to see anyway, but I had a special reason this time. Within the past year he had talked with and later identified two men who were badly wanted. The first time *Life* magazine had run a story and picture on it, and the second time *Look* had done the same thing. Coincidence? Yes and no. A lot of hoods and boosters ended up in that area. I knew from experience.

I sat down, and he brought my drink up. "It's on the house," he said. "How are you, Milo?"

"I'm breathing, which puts me ahead of the game. How's the swill business going?"

"Please," he said with a pained expression. "This is a labor of love. It's not the money that counts—it's the spirits. What was your hurry a minute ago? Important conference in the men's room?"

"I'm being followed. I went out the back door to see who's so interested in me."

"Spot him?"

"Yeah. I couldn't see his face, but he'll be easy to recognize. He's got close-cropped white hair, but his face is much younger-looking."

"I think he's been in here," Bo said. "I think he was in here almost two months ago and then he's been in four or five times in the past three weeks. I don't know his name. He's always been alone and has one drink and leaves. Drinks scotch and water tall. Did you see my picture in *Look?*

"Yeah. If there's one thing I can't stand it's a publicity hound. How come so many wanted men come in here?"

"It's my magnetic charm," he said.

"Is that what they're calling it these days? You'd better be careful or this dive will get the reputation of being the crossroads of the underworld. The FBI will probably want to put an agent on permanent duty in here."

"They'd probably rather have it this way, knowing that I have a keen, alert eye and an infallible memory."

"Careful," I warned, "you're talking about the man you love."

He laughed and went off to wait on some other customers. I lit a cigarette. A moment later he was back. "What are you doing here, Milo?" he asked.

"Just thought I'd drop in and see who's minding the store."

"You're putting me on. Some guy wouldn't be following you if you weren't working."

"I guess you're right. If it were a vacation I'd be followed by broads. But then I wouldn't be getting paid for it."

"I don't know," he said. "I know some broads around here who would follow you and pay you, too."

"Around here, sure. But I can't live on fifty cents a week. Can you keep your mouth shut, Bo?"

"It's painful, but I'll try. What's the scam?"

"I'm working on the Crown case."

He whistled softly. "But that's not an insurance case. How come you're on it?"

"Just lucky, I guess. But my insurance company occasionally gets bitten by the same bug you do—only I'm the one that comes down with the virus."

"What do you mean?"

"Publicity. You'll see soon. They're going to run full-page ads announcing that as a public service they have assigned their best investigator to solve the case and find Crown."

"Your name and all?"

"Heaven forfend! They wanted to and even wanted to run a picture of me in the ad. I told them that I didn't want to be advertised as the Man of Extinction."

"Uh-oh," he said, dropping his voice. "Here comes your friend." He picked up my glass and went to get another drink for me.

I didn't look around. I knew that all I had to do was wait and he'd come into sight. He walked past me and sat about seven stools away so I could see him without even turning my head. He looked around the room, taking in everyone, ending up with a brief, impersonal glance at me. I got a flash of his eyes, which were as strange as his hair. They were a milky blue and completely devoid of any expression.

Bo brought my drink, rang it up, and gave me change. Then he went to wait on the white-haired man and returned with a tall scotch and water.

I didn't want to stare at the man, so I took him in with a number of quick glances. My first thought about the hair and the eyes was that he was an albino, but that wasn't true. His eyebrows were black, and I thought I detected a shadow along his jaw that indicated his beard was also dark. His face was deeply tanned. If I hadn't seen his eyes I probably would have said he was handsome. Before he sat down, I had noticed that he was at least two inches over six feet. He was well dressed but not in the way of the man in the black car who had followed me from Columbus.

Once, when he lifted his glass to take a drink, I noticed the way his coat fell. He was carrying a gun in a shoulder holster. Suddenly I felt naked. My gun was still in my suit-case in the hotel. I probably wouldn't need it, but I would have felt better if I had it. I didn't like the fact that he didn't mind if I saw him.

Bo came back up and talked for a few minutes about the street and several of the people on it. Some of them I knew by sight, others I couldn't place at all, but I nodded as if I knew them all. After a while he had to get back to work.

I sat there, concentrating on my drink, but really brooding over the case. There was something about the attention I was getting that was giving me new things to think about.

Up until then I had been thinking that their interest in me was because I was going in the right direction and they wanted to keep me from finding Crown. I obviously had come in the right direction. I was certain of that. But, I thought, if their chief reason was to keep me from finding Crown, why hadn't they already tried to kill me? The man in the black car could have done it in Athens. The white-haired man could have done it easily when I crossed the street to the bar. I remembered that the street had been relatively empty at the time. He could have shot me from his car and gotten away.

This brought up an interesting possibility. What if they knew that Eugene Crown had come to Los Angeles, or at least this area, and then he had given them the slip? It was just possible they didn't know where he was either. Maybe they were going to stick close to me in the hopes that I would be lucky enough to lead them to him. Then they could, in a manner of speaking, kill two birds with one stone. I made a firm resolve to not go anywhere without my gun after this.

Finally, he finished his drink and walked out without looking at me or anything else. Bo came up almost at once.

"Wasn't that pretty stupid?" he asked. "If he's tailing you, why come in and let you have a look at him? Nobody could forget him once they've seen him."

"I don't think he cares," I said. "He's carrying a gun. I'll bet he knows how to use it, and he knows he does. I also think that all he wants to do at the moment is tag along behind me, and he doesn't even care too much if I know he's there. There's no law against it."

"Know who he is?"

I shook my head. "I know what he is, but that's all."

"Want me to save the glass for you? His fingerprints might be a good thing to have."

I laughed. "There are no fingerprints on that glass. He was careful about that. He picked it up between his thumb and forefinger but far enough back so there won't be any prints. Tomorrow I may be able to find out who he is because I'm sure he's a pro. Now I want to talk to you about Eugene Crown."

"Think everything I had to say was in the story in *Look*."

"I read it, but I want to hear you tell it."

"Well, the first time he came here was about two months ago. It must have been right after he escaped from prison. Except for three days, he was here about two weeks, living in a hotel down the street. He came in here every night and would stay two or three hours, drinking bourbon with water backed. A few times he came in the afternoon, too."

"Did you talk to him at all?"

"Not really," Bo said. "I tried, but he never talked about

much of anything but the weather and sometimes cars. He was crazy about cars. Once in a while he'd say something about a girl at the bar being pretty or a dish. Once he asked how to get to the library. I remembered him when the first pictures came out. That's about it."

"Did he ever make passes at any of the girls?"

Bo shook his head. "I think he wanted to but was afraid. I offered to introduce him to a girl once, but he said he didn't have time."

"Did he ever talk about politics?"

"No."

"How about race relations?"

"No."

"Labor unions?"

"No."

"Did he have plenty of money?"

"Yeah. Even at first he had quite a bit. Then, after he met the man in here, he had a roll."

"What man?" I asked.

"I guess that wasn't in the story," he said. "They must have kept it out. I think it was the third day he was here when this man came in and they left together. It was the next day that Crown went away and didn't come back for three days."

"Where'd he go?"

"I don't know. He didn't say. When he came back he did say something about winning some money, but he didn't say where. One of the reporters told me that the police found out he had been in Vegas. So I guess that's where he was."

"And then what happened?"

"That's all," he said. "He stayed around almost another week and then suddenly took off. That must have been two weeks before the shooting."

I lit a cigarette and looked at Bo. Something about his expression interested me. "When did he come here the second time?"

He looked startled. "How did you know about that? Nothing was printed, and the police told me not to say anything about it."

"So you were going to hold out on your old buddy, huh? Well, give, baby."

He laughed. "He came back the same night the killing took place. It was in the news already, but there was no mention of him. I think it was at least two days later before his name appeared. Anyway he came in here, had a couple of drinks, and then that same man joined him. They went outside for maybe twenty minutes, and Crown came back alone. He looked pretty happy. He stayed around until about midnight and left. I never saw him again. The other man did come in the next night and seemed a little upset when he didn't find Crown here. He left in a hurry, and I haven't seen him since either."

If my latest idea, I thought, was right, that was when he gave them the slip and disappeared. It was an interesting problem. I reached into my pocket and brought out the photograph of Joe Capo.

"Did you ever see this man?" I asked, holding it up.

"Hey," he said, "that's the man. The one who met him here both times. You know who he is?"

"I thought you might recognize him. Yes, I know who he is, but I'm not going to tell you—yet. And I don't want you telling your cop friends that I have the picture or that I know who he is. Is that clear?"

"Yes, Father," he said in mock deference. "Why not, Father?"

"Sooner or later they are going to be swarming all over me anyway. The longer that can be put off, the better. That's one of the aces I have in the hole. I also think I have a slight jump on them, and I want to keep it."

"What kind of aces, Father?"

"You haven't been dealt into the game yet," I said with a smile. "Now I think I'll run along to my little home away from home, and I'll see you tomorrow."

"Why don't you stick around until I close at two, and then we can go have some breakfast and talk?"

I shook my head. "My friend outside will follow us and figure out that we're more than a bartender and customer who are friendly. I don't want you involved at all if possible; if it's not possible, then I don't want you involved yet."

"Okay. Where are you staying?"

"The Continental Hotel. But don't hand it out like giving candy to babies. What time do you get into this dump tomorrow?"

"Well, if I go home and go to sleep right after closing, I should be here by noon. I have to come in and check on everything. Have to watch these thieving bartenders."

"You should know," I said. "I'll phone you sometime after twelve, then." I finished my drink and walked out.

The white-headed man was sitting in his car waiting. I ignored him, got in the Eldorado, and pulled out. I stopped at the corner of Western Avenue and bought a newspaper without getting out of the car. Then I drove straight to the hotel and went upstairs. The first thing I did when I got there was to take my gun and holster out of the suitcase. I made sure the gun was loaded and in working condition, then I slipped it into the holster and hung it on a chair. I didn't think they were going to take a shot at me, but I was too old to enjoy surprise parties.

I called room service and asked for a bucket of ice. I took off my shoes and tie, then hung my jacket over the back of the chair so that the gun wasn't visible. I looked through the paper. Nothing there.

There was a knock on the door. I walked across the room and asked who it was. It was the waiter. I let him in and signed the check. I got the bottle out of my suitcase and made myself a drink. I looked at the bottle and shook my head. "March," I said to myself, "you must be slipping. There was a time when this wouldn't have lasted more than one day."

With a drink in one hand and a cigarette in the other, I sat down to try to think my way through the thickets ahead. I'd had several hours' sleep on the plane and now I was restless and wanting to get ahead with it. There wasn't much to go on, but I felt I had enough insight into Eugene Crown to make some pretty good guesses about what he'd do.

There was only one thing that bothered me. The psychologist at the prison had said there had been a sharp change in Crown just before he broke out. Something must have given him more confidence in himself and made him feel he could stop being a loser. Whatever it was, it must have worked. It was more than two months since he escaped from prison and more than a month since the shooting in Cleveland, and he still hadn't been caught. I was curious about what had caused the change, but I didn't think it made too much difference.

I was also remembering something Ben Crown had told me. He'd said that Eugene had an animal's cunning, especially in regard to traps. If that was true, he must have sensed now that he was in between two traps. His so-called friends were on one side and the law on the other. I'd thought about that when I was talking with Bo. Most animals in that situation would try to make false trails.

There was the matter of that three-day trip he'd taken on his first visit to Los Angeles. According to Bo, a reporter had told him that they'd found out Crown had gone to Las Vegas. Maybe he had, but my hunch said he didn't stay there any longer than it took to establish the fact that he'd been there. Then he'd gone on to wherever he wanted to go.

He had mentioned gambling to Bo. That could have been in Vegas, or it could have been somewhere else, a place where he had some real business. There was a certain amount of gambling all over Nevada, and certain counties in California permitted card rooms, but I ruled these out. It seemed to me that left either Mexico or Reno. Mexico, I felt, was out. He'd have to cross the border, in and out. I decided to take a stab at Reno.

If he had gone there, he might take a fling or two in the casinos, but he'd probably hang out in small neighborhood bars as he had in the past. Anyway, it was worth a try.

If I found out where he'd gone, he certainly wouldn't be there now. So the next question to solve was why he'd gone—wherever it was. The first thing, I was sure because of the new confidence he had exhibited to the psychologist, would be to do something to change his appearance. Not so much to avoid capture as to change the image he'd always had of himself. That would mean plastic surgery, but he'd probably been given enough money so he could handle the expense of that.

Logically, the next thing he'd need would be a passport. Ben had said he was sure that Eugene didn't know where to get such things. But Eugene had served time in a number of prisons, and he must have met a few cons who did know about such things. Some of them must be on the outside by this time. If he knew where to find them …

It was one o'clock in the morning. I phoned room service and asked them to send up a club sandwich and a pot of coffee. By this time I was using paper and pencil, and I'd gotten a map out of my suitcase. The waiter brought the sandwich and coffee. I signed for them and went back to work.

Crown had had plenty of money even on that first trip, according to Bo. If he'd been smart enough to think of laying a false trail, he'd be smart enough to do as good a job of it as possible. Like taking a plane to Vegas, with a round-trip ticket. Then he'd make sure he was seen and remembered in at least one club. Then buy a secondhand car and drive wherever he wanted to go. On the return trip, he could drive the car back to Vegas, sell it, and get on the plane with his return ticket.

I doubted if he could find many plastic surgeons or forgers of passports in Reno, but there was a city fairly near both Reno and Vegas where he could. San Francisco. Then why go to Reno? Maybe there was an ex-con there who had a contact for things like a passport.

I made a circle on the map with the line running through Los Angeles, San Francisco, and Reno. Las Vegas was, of course, inside the circle. Well, it wasn't exactly a circle; it looked more like an egg, but it served its purpose. It meant that he had plenty of time to do all of that in the three days he was away from Los Angeles. With time to spare. He certainly wouldn't need to buy the passport on that first trip. Finding out where he could buy it would be enough.

And he wouldn't—and didn't—have the surgery done on that trip. But he could locate the doctor and make an appointment for one day shortly after the killing of Randolph.

The night he disappeared on the second trip, he could have gone straight to San Francisco, to arrange to get the passport and then go to the doctor for the operation. The whole thing could have been accomplished before Eugene Crown received any publicity in connection with the assassination in Ohio. And shortly thereafter, Eugene Crown—and Shelby Allister—would vanish.

I went over it carefully three or four times, and I thought it stood up. It was a long shot, but I felt it was logical enough to check it out.

By then it was almost three in the morning, and I hadn't touched the sandwich. I realized I was hungry and was glad I'd ordered it. The coffee was cold, so I put the last of the ice in the glass and splashed V.O. into it. It was a fine late snack.

I called downstairs and left a call for eight o'clock. I finished the last drink and the last cigarette. There was only one remaining problem—to leave town without being followed. I had a vague idea about that, so I went to bed and slept on it.

EIGHT

The phone rang, and I groped for it. The operator told me it was eight o'clock. It seemed like I'd just gone to bed. I went in and took a fast shower, which awakened me a little, but I still wasn't quite with it. Despite being an early riser, I was always a slow study when it came to facing a new day.

I phoned room service and ordered a large breakfast, a pot of coffee, and a morning paper. And a bucket of ice. Then I just sat and waited until they came.

First, I made myself a morning drink. After a couple of swallows I finally got my eyes wide open. I lit a cigarette and put in a call to Lieutenant John Rockland in New York City. He came on the phone almost at once.

"Milo," he said, "you called just in time. I've got an early lunch today."

"Whyte's?"

"No such luck. It'll probably be the nearest Greasy Spoon. I'm meeting another lieutenant to talk about coordinating his work on a case with the Special Squad. Where are you?"

"Los Angeles."

"How are you making out?"

"Better than I expected, but not good enough yet. I am making some progress, though."

"You're putting me on," he said. "Since you never make a

local call to me without wanting something, you must want a lot when you make a long-distance call."

"Not much," I said. "I want to describe a man to you. I think he's a pro. Think, hell—I know it. You may know him or have him in the files."

"Go ahead."

"About six feet two inches. I'd guess about two hundred pounds, in his middle or late thirties. His face is well tanned. He has close-cropped snow-white hair, and his eyes are milky blue and bore two holes in you when he looks in your direction."

"Don't have to look in the files," he said. "His name is Samuel Smith, but everyone knows him as Whitey. You're right. He's a pro. He's a gun for the mob, both here and in the Middle West. He also does some freelance work. It is said that he has more notches on his gun than anyone else in the business. Good both with handguns and rifles. Hasn't spent a day in prison since he was eighteen, when they got him on a concealed weapon charge. He's been arrested many times on the charge of assault with a deadly weapon, but he's beaten every rap. Why the sudden interest in him?"

"He's following me so closely you'd think he was in love with me."

"If he's in it," Johnny said, "I guess we're right about its not being a one-man job. And from what I hear, he's high-priced. Well, good luck, chum."

"Thanks, Johnny—and I don't mean for the *mazel tov* bit."*
I hung up and took a couple more swallows from the glass. I
looked at the breakfast. It was covered, so I decided it would
keep warm while I made a phone call to Martin Raymond. I
thought he deserved that much for all the money the company
was spending. I lifted the phone and put in a person-to-person call to him. The call went through the company switchboard, Martin's secretary, and finally he was on.**

"Milo, my boy," he said, "how is everything going?"

"Better than I expected," I said, "but we still have a long
way to go. But I think I've uncovered or guessed a few things
not known to anyone else, and I think I'm one step ahead.
The most encouraging sign is that a few of our less attractive
citizens are becoming interested in me. So I must be more or
less on the right track."

"Good. I knew we could depend on you. Need any more
money?"

"No," I said, feeling very virtuous. "I'll let you know when
I do. I just thought I'd give you a progress report."

"That's thoughtful of you, Milo," he said. (My God, I
thought, our new relationship was getting sickening.) "Where
are you staying, if I want to get in touch with you?"

"The Continental. I'll probably be away for a couple of
days, but I will keep the room while I'm gone."

"Good. We'll wait to hear from you." He hung up.

---

* The Yiddish phrase *mazel tov* literally means "good luck," though usually
it expresses congratulations. Although he is not Jewish, Milo March would be
familiar with common Yiddish expressions popular among New Yorkers (as well
as Angelenos).
** Operator-assisted telephone calls, angst about long-distance rates, ducking into
phone booths—those were the days of Milo March!

I finished my drink and considered the breakfast. Orange juice, scrambled eggs and ham, three slices of toast. I finished all of it and then had two cups of coffee. I began to feel as if the day had really started. All that was missing was dessert. So I poured another drink and went back to the phone. I called the company I'd rented the car from and asked for the man I usually did business with.

"Hello, Mr. March," he said. "Is there something wrong about the car we sent you?"

"No, it's beautiful. So beautiful, in fact, that I want another one."

"You mean instead of the one you have?" He sounded puzzled.

"No. In addition to."

"What are you going to do with two Eldorados, Mr. March?"

"Remember those old *Ben-Hur* movies where the hero drove two chariots at the same time with one foot in each chariot? I thought I'd try the same thing with two Eldorados."

There was a moment of silence, then he realized it was a joke and laughed weakly. But he did try to rally. "That would make quite a picture, Mr. March, but I think the Cadillac people prefer more sedate advertising."

"I expect so," I said. "Do you have a nice, sedate black Eldorado?"

"Yes."

"That's the one I want. Now, listen carefully. I want it delivered tonight about eight o'clock, not later than eight-thirty. Tell the driver to go down Hollywood Boulevard. One block below Wilton Place there's a bar called Casa Del Monte. Tell him to make a left turn on the street that runs beside it and to park the car in the first place he can find that's about a half block from the Boulevard. Then he's to take the keys and the papers into the bar and leave them with the bartender. He's also the owner. Got that?"

"Y-yes. It's a bit unusual, but I understand, Mr. March."

"I expect to use the car tonight. I'll get down there shortly after your man has made the delivery. I'll sign the papers and put the time on them and have my signature and the time witnessed. Then I'll have someone bring the papers up tonight and slip them under the door, or I'll have them sent by special messenger tomorrow morning, whichever you prefer."

"Tomorrow by messenger will be all right." There was another pause, then he continued weakly. "Mr. March, we've had very good relations with you in the past. But this is the most unusual situation I've ever encountered. Are you sure that everything is all right, Mr. March?"

"Quite sure. My company wouldn't like it any other way. It's also necessary to what I'm working on. I'll explain it to you sometime. It'll give you a chuckle."

"I hope so," he said. "The car will be there. Good-bye, Mr. March."

I had another cup of coffee with my drink while I read the morning paper. There was nothing in it about Eugene Crown. I put on a jacket and went down to the lobby and bought a couple of magazines. I went back upstairs and killed the time with the magazines and another drink until it was twelve-thirty. Then I phoned the bar.

"Is Bo there?" I asked when a man answered.

"Who's calling?"

"Tell him Milo wants to talk to him."

In a moment he came on. "What's going on?"

I told him about the car keys that would be brought to him. He was to accept them and give the man who brought them five dollars, which I would return to him when I got there. I told him I'd be there around nine, maybe a little later, and I'd explain about the keys and papers when I got there.

I knew I would get little or no sleep that night, so I'd better get some more sleep that afternoon. I hung a "Do Not Disturb" sign on the door, had a couple more drinks—which practically finished the bottle—and stretched out on the bed. I fell asleep quicker than I thought I would.

It was a few minutes past six when I awakened. I shaved and got dressed. I had decided not to take any clothes with me. I couldn't get them in and out of the car without Whitey Smith seeing me. I would buy what I needed on the trip. I went downstairs and had a good steak dinner, taking my time over it. I then told the clerk at the desk that I would probably be out of town for a couple of days but was keeping the suite. I went outside and waited for the white Eldorado.

As I pulled into the street, I saw a car fall in behind me. So I had my escort.

It was twenty minutes past nine when I parked in front of the bar. I saw him park a few cars back of me, but I paid no attention and went inside. Again I sat at the end of the bar. Bo came up with the keys, the papers, and a drink for me. I put six dollars on the bar.

"What's going on?" he asked again.

"I'll tell you in a minute." I went through the papers, marking the time on each one and signing it. Then I had Bo witness them. I slipped them into the envelope that had come with them and sealed it. I took another five dollars from my pocket and handed both to Bo. "Tomorrow I want you to send this envelope by special messenger. The five should cover it and the tip. The address is printed on the envelope."

"Okay."

"Is there a place where you live that you can park a car?"

"Yes."

"The white Eldorado is parked out front," I said. "Here are the keys. Take it home with you. You can take a joyride or two, but don't try to see how fast it'll go. This might involve you, but I don't think so."

"What do you mean?"

"I'm going out of town, and I'm going to give my white-headed friend the slip—I hope. I'll leave as soon as I have this one drink. He'll probably come in here in an hour or so for a drink and to check on me. He'll flip when he sees I'm not here. If he asks you about me, just tell him that you don't know where I went. He'll probably go out and comb the other bars, but I doubt if he'll stake the car out. Not as late as two in the morning. So you take the car and stash it. Out of sight if possible."

"Where are you going?"

"For a ride," I said with a smile. "I may call you tomorrow night." I finished my drink.

"I see you're carrying a little armor yourself tonight."

"Sure," I said. "You can never tell when I'll be invited to a come-as-you-are party. I want to be ready. See you on the way back, Bo."

I went out through the rear door and turned to the right. I found the black Eldorado some fifty yards up the street. I drove straight up to Franklin, then hit Los Feliz to the Golden State Freeway. From it, I branched off onto Route 395. I had been watching carefully, and no one was following me. I was on my way.

By five o'clock I was entering Reno. The only stops I'd made had been for gas, and there had been little traffic on the road. I decided not to check into a motel yet. Almost everything was open twenty-four hours a day. There were one or two people I wanted to see. This way I'd have a chance to check on when I could catch them and also have some breakfast. I could always sleep later.

I parked on Second Street just off Virginia and went into a bar called The Sewer. It was just a bar, no gambling. Oh, there were two slot machines, but that's not really gambling. There were four or five people at the bar; I couldn't tell the number for sure because the light was so dim. Two of them were asleep with their heads on the bar.

The bartender wasn't anyone I recognized. I ordered a gin and grapefruit juice and waited until he had served it and brought my change.

"Who's working the morning shift?" I asked. "Teddie?" He was the owner.

"No. Kenny's working. Jack Kenny." He was the other one I knew there.

"He comes on at eight?"

"No. The hours have been shifted around. The day shift starts at ten now. You from around here?"

I shook my head. "New York. I was here last year. I've just been in L.A. and thought I'd drop up and see how everyone was."

"About the same, I guess," he said. "Teddie'll probably be in before noon."

"I'll try to catch him and Kenny at about the same time," I said. I finished my drink and had another one. Then I went down the street to the Cal-Neva and had some breakfast. Since I couldn't see the two men I wanted to, I decided to rack up two or three hours of sleep. I changed my mind about a motel, too. I went back to the car and drove a couple of blocks to the Holiday. I checked in, left a call for nine-thirty, and went to sleep.

The operator awakened me at nine-thirty. I washed my face, straightened my tie, and went downstairs. I had two cups of coffee and then walked to Second Street and into The Sewer.

Jack Kenny was tending bar. He was a big man, over six feet, about thirty-five. He looked and moved like a retired fighter. Maybe not so retired. I knew that I would rather have him on my side than on the other side. I had only met him the time I'd been in Reno before, but we understood each other. He was one of the few people I would have trusted to watch my back for me in trouble.

He caught the sight of me as I sat down at the end of the bar. He came over with a big smile on his face, his hand stretched out.

"Milo March," he said. "When did you get in town?"

I shook hands with him. "About five this morning. No one was around, so I had some breakfast and caught three hours' sleep at the Holiday. How's everything with you?"

"Not bad. You still drinking gin and grapefruit juice?"

"Once in a while."

He mixed me a drink, even remembering to use the rock glass, and put it in front of me. "That's on me," he said.

"My father," I said gravely, "taught me never to say no to a woman or a drink." I raised the glass. "Cheers."

He nodded. "Staying long?"

"A day or two is all. Someday I'm going to take a vacation and spend it all right here."

"Keeping you busy?"

"Yeah. Which reminds me—" I pulled the two pictures from my pocket. I had cut all the printed matter from the picture of Crown. I handed it over. "Ever see this man around here?"

"About two months ago he was here for a couple of days. Spent most of them here." He smiled. "I've also seen his picture in the papers. He's wanted on the murder of that politician in Ohio, isn't he?"

"That's the boy. Got any idea what he was doing in Reno?"

"He didn't talk much. Or, rather, he talked, but he didn't say much. He did seem to know one of our local citizens and was in here drinking with him both days. Maybe he just came to cut up old touches with this guy."

"Know who he is?"

"Sure. He's one of our regular customers. He's an old ex-con named Bernie Shale. I think he's been clean for several years, though. He lives here and works at odd jobs, usually dish-washing or cleaning up bars."

"How long has he been out?"

"Seven or eight years, I guess. He never talks about it." Then he dropped his voice. "Here he comes now."

I kept looking straight ahead, and then a small, stooped man shuffled into view. His hair was white, and his face had more lines in it than a crossword puzzle. He took a stool at the middle of the bar and pulled a letter from his pocket.

Kenny had already opened a bottle of beer and was taking it and a glass down to him. He put it down and said something. The old man looked up and smiled. He put some coins on the bar and took the letter from the envelope.

After ringing up the money, Kenny came back to me. "Maybe I'm wrong about him being retired. Somebody's send-ing him money by mail."

I had a sudden hunch. "Kenny, see if you can read where it was mailed from. He's put the envelope on the bar."

Kenny nodded and moved slowly down the bar. He stopped for a minute and said something to the old man again. He was answered with another smile and a nod of his head. Kenny went on down the bar and then turned and came back up.

"Portugal," he said. "There's no return address on it. Mean anything?"

"I think so, but I won't know for sure until later." I finished my drink. "Give me another and have one yourself."

"Don't mind if I do," he said. He made the drinks and

collected the money. "Have something to do with that Crown business?" he asked.

"I think so."

"I hope he isn't in it too far. He's a nice old guy, and I'd hate to see him have to go up again."

"If it's what I think it is, there's no need for him to come into the picture at all." Out of the corner of my eyes, I saw that the owner of The Sewer had just come in with his wife. "By the way," I went on, "how's that cheap boss of yours?" Then I pretended to see him for the first time. "Hello, Crooked Ted. Hello, Arlene. Are you still putting up with him?" She laughed and twinkled her eyes at me.

"Hello, Sherlock Holmes," he said. "What are you doing here?"

"Somebody wrote and told me you were having trouble keeping the store open, so I thought I'd come over and buy a couple of drinks. That ought to double your gross."

"Just about."

"Kenny," I said, "give your boss and his boss a drink."

"I thought you'd never ask," Teddie said. "But you have, so I'll choke one down."

Kenny brought two beers and took the money from me. I looked at the bottle of beer, then leaned closer for a better look. "I've been robbed."

"What's the matter with you?"

"I've been tricked into buying someone a near beer. If word of that ever gets back to Madison Avenue, I'll be ruined." Just then I noticed that Bernie Shale was sliding off the stool and starting to leave. I waited a couple of minutes after he went out, finishing my drink, then I got up. "See you later," I said.

When I got outside, I didn't see him anywhere. I was standing there, looking around and wondering which direction to try, when he came out of the liquor store next door. There was a package under his arm, so I guessed he was planning on doing the rest of his drinking at home. He trudged down the street, and I followed—at a distance.

We covered about eight blocks before he finally turned in at a house. I walked on by. It was an old house with a "Rooms for Rent" sign on the front. I turned and retraced my steps, stopping once to write down his name and the address of the house.

I felt pretty good about the results of my guesswork of two nights back in Los Angeles. I felt anxious to get back to work.

NINE

By the time I reached The Sewer, I'd made up my mind not to stay over in Reno until the next day. I would leave for San Francisco right after lunch. I sat in the same spot and ordered another drink. The place was beginning to fill up, but everyone had drinks in front of them, so Kenny stayed when he gave me the drink.

"Find out where he lived?" he asked.

I nodded.

"I knew that's why you went out. I thought of something else while you were gone. I'd forgotten all about it until after you brought up Crown. It must've been three or four months ago that a letter came here for old Bernie. Even he was surprised when I handed it to him. He never said anything about it, just read it and put it in his pocket. But the thing I remembered was that there wasn't any return address on the envelope, but up in that corner there was a rough drawing of a crown."

"Crown was in the slammer then," I said, "but he might have written it."

"Another thing. The writing on the envelope was in pencil. And it was the kind of cheap paper a guy in the joint could get. It had been folded, so Crown probably got some guy to smuggle it outside. It happens every day."

"I know," I said. "You're probably right. Thanks, Kenny."

"Okay." He hesitated a minute. "But just don't hurt the old man too much. I doubt if he did anything too serious and probably didn't know what Crown was mixed up in. If he ever goes back to the can, he'll never come out alive. I think he deserves at least to die on the outside."

"I won't hurt him at all," I said. "I have an idea I'm going to end up being very grateful to him."

I had one more drink, then left. I told Kenny I might see him when the case was over. First, I went shopping and bought some shirts, shorts, and socks. While I was at it, I also bought a small bag. On the way back to the hotel, I stopped in a drugstore and bought a toothbrush, toothpaste, a razor and blades, and shaving soap. When I got back to my room I shaved and showered and changed clothes. I packed everything else into the new bag I'd bought. Then I went downstairs to the dining room, where I had one dry martini and a fine lunch. Then I had a boy bring my bag down, paid the bill, got in the Eldorado, and headed for San Francisco.

It was still early evening when I reached the city. I drove downtown and stopped at the first good-looking hotel I saw. I checked in and then took a taxi to Chinatown. I walked around for a while, then went to Herman Po's restaurant.

Herman Po was the cousin of one of the most engaging rascals I'd ever met—Po Hing of Hong Kong. It was Po Hing who had sent me to his cousin a couple of years before when I needed some special services in the States.* It was still early, so the restaurant was less than half full. I took an empty booth fairly well removed from the other diners.

---

* See *A Man in the Middle* by M.E. Chaber. Po Hing first appeared in *Jade for a Lady*.

"I'll have a dry martini," I told the waiter when he came. "And will you tell Herman Po that one of his brothers is here and would like to speak with him?"

The waiter merely nodded his head, showing no surprise, and hurried away. It wasn't much later when he returned with the martini and left without saying anything.

I was halfway through my martini when I saw him coming, looking like a cherubic Buddha—if there is such a thing—in a Madison Avenue suit. He stopped to speak to several customers and finally arrived at my table.

"The House of Po," he said in Cantonese, "is honored to have a brother as our guest. And how is March *hsien* tonight?"

"It is I who am honored by your presence," I said in the same language. Then I switched to English. "I'm fine. Won't you sit down and join me in a drink?"

"Why not?" he asked as he sat down. He was barely down when a waiter appeared with a drink and put it in front of him. "I really dig that old way of speaking, but if Po Hing were here, he'd say we were both squares. Have you seen my illustrious cousin recently?"

"Not since the last time I saw you. But I never know when I might go there again."

"We do as it is willed," he said, shrugging. "I gather that you have some business in San Francisco."

"You gather well. I wish to buy some information if it is possible."

"So?"

"I don't imagine there are many artists in San Francisco who do such delicate work as passports?"

He smiled. "Not many."

I took from my pocket the picture of Eugene Crown. "I have reason to believe that this man, with his face slightly altered perhaps, inquired about such a work of art and finally obtained one about four weeks ago. It is possible that he inquired as long ago as eight weeks, when he did look like this. I think that when he finally completed the transaction, his ears were less prominent and the scar on his face was gone." I passed the picture over to him.

He glanced at it. "May I keep this?"

"Yes. I have another one."

"It is possible I can find out for you. The cost will be between five hundred and a thousand dollars. If I am successful, I will have the information by tomorrow night."

"A thousand will be all right," I said. "I'll give it to you now."

"Not necessary. The man will trust me and I trust you. Payment will be made when you receive the information. I see my brother is armed against the evil elements. You are expecting trouble?"

"I always expect trouble," I said with a smile. "It is the best spell I know to cast against evil spirits."

"It is true," he said gravely. "I thank my brother for the drink, and I will see him here tomorrow night."

"I'll be here."

He stood up and walked away toward the back of the restaurant. I had another martini and then a fine dinner. When I had started to order, the waiter had told me that Herman Po had already ordered it for me. I was glad he had. After dinner I walked around Chinatown for a while, then took a taxi to the hotel. Up in my room, I called room service and told them to send up a bottle of V.O., some ice, and all the newspapers that were available. I took off my jacket and tie and hung my gun in the closet while waiting.

There was a knock on the door. I opened it and the waiter came in with my order. I signed the check, and soon as he was gone I removed my shoes, slacks, and shirt. It was going to be a nice, quiet evening at home for March. Except for reading the papers, I wasn't even going to think about the case.

I made a drink and skimmed through the papers rapidly. No mention of Crown. So then I leaned back and read the comics, the sports, and part of the front-page news. I even read some of "Dear Abby" just to prove that I was open-minded, but it didn't come up to the love lives of Li'l Abner and Daisy. Then I turned on television and really began to relax. I watched the idiot box until midnight and went to sleep.

I was awake by eight in the morning. I ordered breakfast and turned the television on for the news. The breakfast came—different this time because I had ordered sausages instead of ham. Every once in a while I get daring. I had my usual one morning drink, to rinse the sleep away from my brain, and ate breakfast.

By the time I'd finished dressing, it was late enough so that I could start making phone calls. I got some paper and a pencil from the desk and phoned the AMA, asking for a list of plastic surgeons in the city. They gave it to me. It was a little longer than I had expected, but I wrote them all down.

Since I didn't know the streets too well, I decided to leave the Eldorado in the hotel garage and take a taxi. I explained to the driver that I had a number of places to go but I wouldn't be long, and I would want him to wait for me. He didn't mind; he could already hear that meter clicking. So we started off. At each place I would show the doctor my ID, then the picture of Crown, and ask the same questions.

I finally hit pay dirt at the eighth office. It belonged to a Dr. Francis Blair. He turned out to be a small, bald-headed man with the expression of a person who has just lost something. He peered at me through thick glasses as though searching for the blemish I wanted removed.

"I'm not a patient," I told him for the second time. "I am an insurance investigator for the Intercontinental Insurance Company."

That penetrated. "Intercontinental?" he said. "A very fine company. But I already have several policies with them, so—"

"I'm not selling insurance," I said, resisting the temptation to shout it. "I'm an *investigator* for them. I want to ask you about someone who may have been your patient."

"A patient of mine? Who?"

"This one," I said, putting the photograph of Crown in front of his glasses.

He started nodding his head, and a smile came on his face. "A very interesting young man. He'd had all sorts of complexes because of those ears and that scar. Terrible. I did a beautiful job for him. He went out of here a new man. Yes, sir. I asked him to keep in touch with me and let me know how his life changed. I want to do a paper on him."

"Sounds like a good idea," I said. "What was his name?"

"You don't know?"

"No. I know what he looks like—or what he did look like. But I don't know his name."

"Come. I will look it up."

I followed him into the office. One wall was covered with filing cabinets. He opened one drawer and took out a folder. He looked in it. "The operation was done four weeks and three days ago. His name is Hamilton Throne. There."

"Do you operate here?"

"Usually. There's an operating room just back of this office. For him it was a very simple operation. It should have been done years ago. Think of all those wasted years."

"I am," I said. "He paid for the operation?"

"In cash. Before the operation. A fine young man."

"I can see that. So you did a good job on him?"

"Beautiful. Here, I will show you." He opened the folder and took out a large glossy photograph. On it there were two pictures. "Before and after," he announced triumphantly.

It took me a minute to realize that they were two pictures of the same man. The one on the left was undoubtedly Eugene Crown, but the one on the right looked like a different man. It was only when you looked closely that you could see it was also Crown. The name Hamilton Throne was typed on the bottom with a Los Angeles address. I recognized the number as being that of a hotel on Hollywood Boulevard. So I could forget that.

"That is remarkable," I said.

"You bet," he said. "I do beautiful work, so you come to me. 'If you want to be fair, you come to Doctor Blair.' You sure you don't have some little blemish that you want removed?"

"Quite sure. I'm too pretty as it is. ... Look, Doctor, could I get a copy of that 'after' picture?"

"Please," he said, drawing himself up to his full five feet two inches. "There is such a thing as medical ethics. What you ask is unthinkable. The relationship between a doctor and his patient is as sacred as that between a priest and a member of his flock. Remember that, young man, or I shall report you to your president. I went to school with good old—now, what's his name?"

"His name," I said wearily, "is J.B. Throckmorton." I remembered hearing it once, that was all.

"That's what I said. I shall report you to good old Throcky."

"Throcky?"

"That's what we called him at school. A man of steel was good old Throcky."

"Well," I said weakly, "thank you very much, Doctor. I shall see to it that your confidences are respected."

"Thank you, young man. It is what I would expect from anyone who works for Throcky. I always—"

I didn't wait to hear what it was that he always did. I was out the door and managed to reach the elevator before I exploded with laughter. Throcky! I had to file that away in my memory bank.

Still, it had been a successful morning. I did have one new name for Crown, but I suspected it wasn't worth much. It would be good, however, to have my guess verified. The only thing missing was a photograph of the "new" Eugene Crown. Maybe, I thought as I started laughing again, Throcky could get it for us.

It was noon, so I had the taxi driver take me to one of the better restaurants for lunch. I felt I had earned it. I treated myself to a jumbo-size martini at the bar.

I was on my second martini when the idea came to me. "Milo, my boy," I said to myself in imitation of Martin Raymond, "I think it might be safe to now say we have a slight edge on all those bloodhounds. If our luck holds up, we just might pull off the whole thing to the glory of dear old Intercontinental—and dear old Throcky, of course."

The lunch brought further happiness to me. I took a taxi back to the hotel. I picked up all the newspapers, including the *New York Times* and the *Christian Science Monitor,* and went on to my room. I removed my coat and kicked off my shoes. I piled the pillows together on the bed, fixed myself a drink, lit a cigarette, and was ready to go to work.

I found one short item in three of the papers. It said that reports were now coming into the FBI by the thousands, and Eugene Crown had been seen boarding a plane for almost every country in the world. It quoted one right-wing leader who declared he had proof that Crown was a Communist and was already safely in Russia. At the end of the story it stated that the FBI was promising an early arrest.

I decided to take a nap. If I was still lucky and Herman Po got anything for me, I might leave for Los Angeles right after dinner. So a nap would come in handy.

When I awakened it was five o'clock. I went into the bathroom and washed my face, checking to see if I needed another shave. I didn't, so I changed shirts, knotted my tie, strapped on the gun, and shrugged into my coat. I was ready to go.

I took a taxi to Herman's restaurant and went upstairs. Only a few booths were occupied. I chose one and sat down. In a few minutes one of the waiters came over.

"Boss say to serve you drink. He be out soon. What you like to drink?"

"Dry martini," I said.

He scurried away and soon came back with it. I lit a cigarette and sipped on the drink. It was probably fifteen minutes before Herman appeared. The waiter reached the table the same time Herman did, and his drink was in front of him by the time he sat down.

"Got a new cook in the kitchen who just tried to pretend he's the boss," he said. "I had to take a few minutes to give him religion. Sorry."

"No rush," I said. "Relax."

He smiled. "Venerable ancestors once said that man who hurries is always late. I've got news for you. The man you're interested in did come here, first about eight weeks ago. He got in touch with a certain man, and he was recommended by someone who this man once did much work for. Your man said that he didn't need it for another month but wanted to be sure he could get it. He also wanted to know how much it would cost. The price was two thousand dollars. He said that would be all right and he would return in a month."

"That fits," I said.

"He came back exactly four weeks ago. He told my man what he wanted and said that he could do the work at once, except for the photograph, which would have to wait for four or five days. He paid half the fee and said he'd be back in four or five days for the photograph and would pay the remainder then."

I shook my head. I saw the expression on Herman's face and hastened to explain. "That fits. I was shaking my head only because it is surprising." It was, too. Eugene Crown, the loser, had suddenly started acting like a winner.

"Well," Herman said, "he came back on time. His appearance had changed. Where the scar had once been, there was only a shadow. The ears looked all right, but they were flat to the head where once they had spread like the wings of a bat. My friend took the picture, airbrushed away the shadow on the cheek, and fixed it to the passport. My friend, you understand, is an artist. He did not have to ask questions. He knew there had been plastic surgery and that the shadow would disappear—so he made it disappear. He received his money, and the client vanished at once."

"What was the name on the passport?"

"It was a Belgian passport, and the name on it was Lance Copper, a naturalized citizen of Belgium who lived in Brussels."

It was smart. I wondered how much was Crown's idea and how much the forger's. And there was a new name. This now made four names for Crown.

"It is good," I said. "Well worth the fee, whatever it is."

"Wait, my brother," Herman said. "You also get a bonus. In fact, two of them. Because of this, although it was not asked, I told him that he would be paid one thousand dollars."

"That's all right."

"First," Herman said carefully, "the client wanted certain

other papers. They concerned entry into the country of Portugal."

I must admit that I stopped and looked at the sheer beauty of it. Portugal was one of the places you could buy almost anything. So Lance Copper could go there and then reappear under another name and go on to another country. If plastic surgery had made Eugene Crown this clever, maybe I should go in for it myself. I smiled at the thought.

"I see," said Herman, "that my younger brother has reached the correct thought concerning this. Now, as part of this bonus, I give you the name of a man in Lisbon who is as much an artist as is my friend. It is written on a slip of paper, as is the name of my friend, which I will give you. The address is not available, but you should be able to find him without trouble. Thus you will learn the next step."

"Herman," I said, "my brother, you are a jewel beyond compare."

"There is more," Herman said. He pulled a photograph from his pocket. "This is an enlarged picture from the negative that was made for the passport." He slid it across to me. It was pretty much the same picture I had seen in the doctor's office. I put it in my pocket.

"Herman," I said, "you don't know how much you have done for me. I don't know how I can ever repay you."

"Brothers," he said, "exist to help other brothers. I may joke about my cousin Po Hing, but he does not bestow the mark of brotherhood on anyone lightly. That is the way he is one with our ancestors."

Underneath the table, I counted out fifteen hundred dollars.

I checked the room, and no one was paying any attention to us. I passed the money to Herman.

"There is additional money there," I said.

"I will see that it is passed to my friend," he said. He slid a slip of paper across to me. I put it in my pocket.

"Now, what can I do for my brother who has given me so much?"

He smiled. "Brothers do not take pay from brothers. There may come a time when things are such that you feel the need to give to me. That is different. I expect you will leave soon?"

I nodded. "Right after dinner, I think. This information is too valuable to just sit on it. I am eternally grateful to you."

He waved one pudgy hand. "It was nothing. If you do get to Hong Kong, tell Hing that I said hello."

"I will," I promised.

He walked away. I beckoned the waiter and told him I would have another martini and would then order. He said that Mr. Po had already ordered for me. He left, then returned with the food just as I reached the bottom of my glass. It was different than the dinner the night before but equally good, with many dishes I'd never tasted before.

After dinner I went straight back to the hotel. I packed my bag and had it taken downstairs. I paid my bill, and by that time the Eldorado was out front. A moment later I was on my way south.

It was one o'clock in the morning when I reached Hollywood. I drove to the Casa Del Monte. I didn't see any sign of the car that Whitey Smith had been driving. The white Eldorado was there in front of the bar. I parked behind it and went inside. There were only a few diehards at the bar. I sat in my usual place, and Bo brought me a drink without being asked.

"When did you get back?" he asked.

"Just now."

"How did it go?"

"Good, I think."

"That's all?" he asked, a wounded look on his face.

I smiled. "That's all for now. When it's over, I'll come back and tell you the whole story. What's new here?"

"The FBI is looking for you."

TEN

The expected had finally happened. I'd known that sooner or later they'd find out I was working on the case and be looking me up. I wondered where they'd got the word. I was sure it wasn't from either Reno or San Francisco. I thought it was probably from Columbus.

"When?" I asked.

"They were here yesterday afternoon and again last night. They'll probably be dropping in today."

"Okay. I have to see them sometime, so it might as well be now as later."

"They asked me if I knew where you lived, and I said I didn't but that you usually came in at least once a day. I left it at that."

"Good. What about Whitey Smith?"

He laughed. "He came in about thirty minutes after you left. First he looked surprised, and then he looked mad. He didn't ask me anything but just whirled around and left. He came back once later and just looked in. I haven't seen him since."

"I guess he finally admitted to himself that he'd lost me and is now staked out at the hotel waiting for me to show up. But I'll also bet he made a few phone calls. How did you like the Eldorado?"

"Groovy," he said. "I think I'll start putting my pennies in a piggy bank so I can buy one."

"They'll probably have a better model out by then," I said with a laugh.

"Yeah, but there's a fringe benefit in it. If I'm ever completely broke, I can break the piggy bank and get enough out to buy a drink."

"I hadn't thought of that. ... What time do they start handing out tickets on the Boulevard?"

"Nine, I think."

"I'm taking this car back first thing in the morning. Give me the keys to the white car, and I'll pick it up then."

"Okay." He pulled the keys from his pocket and gave them to me. "I saw your company's ad in a magazine today. Have you seen it?"

I shook my head. "Afraid to. I might cry. You'll be in tomorrow afternoon?"

"I guess so. I usually am."

I'll be around then," I said. I finished my drink. "I'll see you."

I went out and drove to the hotel. I stopped in the lobby to get a morning newspaper, then went on to my room. It looked the same as when I'd left it. I got undressed and poured myself a drink—without ice. I sat on the couch with the drink and a cigarette and started going through the paper. Nothing about Crown. I was so tired that I almost missed a story that did interest me. It was a small story on page 3.

The headline was "Shooting on Wilton Place." The story said that a Joseph Capo, alleged racketeer, had been driving south on Wilton Place when another car passed him. Three shots had been fired from the passing car, one hitting Capo in the shoulder, one grazing his neck, and one missing him. Capo had been released from General Hospital after being treated for his wounds. He told the police that he didn't know who could have been shooting at him, and the only description he could give was that it had been a small black car.

The last time I had seen Whitey Smith, he was driving a black Corvette. It was very interesting.

Why Capo? He must have been Crown's contact. Was it because they didn't know where Crown was or who would find him? If they couldn't kill Crown, the next best thing would be to kill the one link between him and whoever was putting out all that money. It made sense—their kind of sense.

I left a call with the operator for seven forty-five and an order with room service for a pot of coffee at eight and went to sleep.

The call awakened me right on time. I washed some of the sleep out of my eyes, saw that I needed a shave, and then the waiter was knocking on the door with the pot of coffee. I poured a cup partly full and then laced it with V.O.

I went to the phone and put in a call to Martin Raymond in New York. After a lot of talk between the operator and Intercontinental personnel, he answered the phone.

"Milo, my boy, where are you?"

"Still in Los Angeles."

"How's it going?"

"Pretty good, I think. I'll be in New York tomorrow and will tell you about it. I just wanted to alert you that I will need more money then."

"We'll have it ready for you. When will you be here?"

"In the morning, I expect. I'll try to get on a plane tonight. In the meantime, have your secretary make reservations for me for day after tomorrow on the plane for Lisbon."

"Lisbon, eh?" he said. I could tell he was dying of curiosity. "All right, Milo. Have you seen our ad?"

"No. I've been too busy."

"We're getting a great response to it. Been getting phone calls ever since it appeared, plus quite a number of tele-grams."

"I'm thrilled for you, Martin," I said dryly. "I'll see you tomorrow." I hung up.

After I'd finished the cup of coffee, I phoned the airport and got a reservation on an eleven o'clock flight that night. I had another cup of coffee and then shaved and got dressed.

I couldn't be certain of it, but I didn't think I was followed as I drove to the car rental place on Santa Monica. I left the car with them and took a taxi to the Casa Del Monte. There wasn't a ticket on the white Eldorado, but I was just in time. A meter maid was coming up the street. I got in the car and drove uptown to a place where I could have a good breakfast.

One of the cars behind me could have been following me, but I didn't spot the Corvette or anybody who looked like Whitey. I was curious about him. I had been sure he'd be outside the hotel every morning until I appeared.

I had a long, leisurely breakfast, then drove to the Holly-wood Public Library, where I spent the next hour or so doing some research. By the time I'd finished that, it was almost noon. I drove back down to the Casa Del Monte. When I got out of the car I saw that Whitey was parked across the street. It wasn't the Corvette, but there was no mistaking Whitey.

I took my usual seat at the bar and ordered a drink. I saw that Bo wasn't there yet. There were a few men at the other end of the bar, and there were several people at the tables having lunch.

I was almost finished with my drink when Bo came in. He said hello and went on down the bar. I saw him stop to speak to one of the men, then he went behind the bar. He looked at me and rolled his eyes toward the group of men back of him. I knew it was supposed to mean something, but I wasn't sure what. I soon found out.

I had just ordered a drink when one of the men detached himself from the others and walked up front. He was about thirty years old, dressed casually, and looked like a young executive. I thought he was leaving, but he wasn't. He came up and took the stool next to me. "Hello, March," he said. I already knew the answer, but I played it straight. "Hello," I said. I looked at him. "Do I know you?"

"You do now," he said pleasantly. He took a card case from his pocket and opened it. "FBI."

"Hello, FBI," I said. "Are you always called that, or do you have a name of your own?"

"Andrews."

"Hello, Andy," I said. "Can I buy you a drink?"

"I don't drink on duty."

"Oh?" I said. "You had a drink in front of you when I came in. Did you just go on duty when I entered?"

He didn't look too happy, but he decided to ignore that question. "I see you're carrying a gun."

"Go to the head of the class," I said. I unbuttoned my jacket and threw it open. "A beautiful gun, isn't it? I also have a beautiful permit to go with it. Do you want to see it?"

He gave me a tight smile. "No. I was told that you had several gun permits." He was going to be polite if it killed him. That was one thing about the FBI—they were always polite until they were certain it was all right to be impolite. "What are you doing in Los Angeles, March? On a case?"

I motioned to the bartender, who came over at once although he did look a little nervous. "Give me another drink. And give my friend here a Coke. I think his mouth is getting a little dry." I waited until the bartender left and then looked at him. His face was slightly pinker than it had been. "You asked me a question. ... Oh, yes. Am I on a case? I'm always on a case when I'm out of New York City."

"What's the case? Eugene Crown?"

The bartender brought the drinks and took my money. I waited until he had left. "I'm surprised at you, Andy. You should know better than to ask a question like that." I remembered the plastic surgeon in San Francisco. "My relationship to a case I'm working on is the same as a priest's relationship to a confession he's just received." I could almost hear his teeth grinding.

"I was warned about you," he said tightly. "You're supposed to have important connections in Washington. That won't keep us from pulling you in."

"On what charge, Andy?"

"Obstructing justice."

"For example?"

"We know that you're working on the Eugene Crown case. We know that you talked to the psychologist in the prison at Columbus, Ohio."

"Sheer natural curiosity. I was there on business and I asked a few questions about Crown. What else?"

"Where were you for the last two days?"

"I went to visit a very sick old aunt in Sacramento. I'm her favorite nephew. Is there something illegal about that?"

"Rubbish," he said. "At the moment, I don't have anything I can arrest you for, but I want you to know that we won't tolerate any amateur messing into this case."

I looked him over. "You won't, eh? I admit that I don't have a degree in law or even in accounting, but I'm a pro, baby. I've solved more cases than you've had assigned to you. Any kind of cases."

"Maybe you have," he said. "That has nothing to do with what we're talking about. If I find you digging into the Crown case, I'll pull you in, and I don't care if military intelligence considers you some kind of sacred cow."

"Please," I said, "not cow. If you're going to call me names like that, make it a sacred bull. I can get testimonial letters for you if you insist."

He chose to ignore that, too. "I saw the ad your company is running everywhere, bragging how they assigned their best investigator to look into the Crown case. I guess that's you, huh?"

"Would you put that in writing? I might get a raise out of it. Relax, junior. I'm leaving for New York City tonight at eleven o'clock. By plane. Somebody else in the Bureau will have to worry about me."

"Why are you going to New York? Is that where you think Crown is?"

"No," I said. "That's where my home office is. The company is narrow-minded about one thing; they insist that I show up in the office once in a while."

"All right, March. Just keep in line and there won't be any trouble." He got up and started to leave.

"Andy," I said, "you forgot your Coke."

He looked at me, and for a minute I thought he was going to tell me what to do with the Coke. But he closed his mouth and went on back to the public phone in the rear. When he'd finished making his phone call, he looked angrier than ever. I would have bet he just found out I did have a plane reservation. On his way back, he stopped to say something to the men he'd been sitting with, and then he went out through the front door without looking at me.

I went back to my drink, then became aware that one of the other men was coming in my direction. He stopped beside me. There was a faint smile on his face.

"Mr. March," he said, "I'm Peterson of the *Times*. Would you care to make a statement about your conversation with Special Agent Andrews?"

"Yes," I said gravely. "You may quote me as saying that I'm very fond of Los Angeles and always come here when I have any spare time. You may also say that I am very fond of the Bureau and especially of Special Agent Andrews, and that I think he and the rest of the agents are doing a splendid job of protecting us. Oh, yes, you can add that I consider the Casa Del Monte one of the finest bars in the country."

He laughed. "Thank you, Mr. March."

"You're welcome," I said. "Are the other gentlemen with you from the press?"

"Yes. They're from the networks, except for one man who's from the *New York Times*."

"Thank you," I said. I raised my voice. "Bo!"

"Yeah?" he said.

"Give all those gentlemen down there a drink on me." The *Times* man went back to his stool as Bo told the bartender. I raised my own empty glass as Bo looked in my direction, and he came to serve me himself.

"What was that all about?" he asked as I put my money on the bar.

"A friendly chat between the agent and myself," I said. "He seemed to think I was poaching on their territory. I assured him that I was not and that by late tonight I would be out of his district and somebody else would have to worry about me."

"Is that why he looked so angry?"

"I don't know the answer to that. Maybe the boy has domestic problems, or maybe somebody chewed him out this morning."

I noticed that the newsmen were laughing as the bartender served their drinks. They looked at me and all of them raised their glasses. "Cheers," the *Times* man said.

I lifted my own glass. "May all your assets be liquid," I called out.

"Are you really leaving town tonight?" Bo asked.

"Yeah. Eleven o'clock."

"Where are you going?"

"New York."

"Why?"

"That's where my home office is," I said seriously.

"I know," he said. "Then what are you going to do?"

"I don't really know. I'm a little tired. I might even take a short holiday."

He cursed under his breath. "Okay, okay. When are you going to tell me about it?"

"As soon as I come back from the holiday. I promise, Bo."

"Okay," he said grumpily.

"Stop worrying. I'll be back. It won't hurt you to wait. And as far as I know, you may talk in your sleep. After this, stop identifying people and you won't have to be so curious."

He laughed. "Then tell them to stop coming into my bar."

I shook my head. "That would make my job harder. I'd have to start going around to bar after bar trying to find out where they had been going."

"What are you going to do now?" he asked.

"Loaf until it's time to catch the plane."

"Have a drink on the house," he said, "and wait about ten minutes. Then I'll take you down the street and buy you a drink—just so you can see how superior this joint is."

"Whitey Smith is out front."

"So what? He's interested in you, not me. It'll do you good to see how the other half lives."

I nodded and he went to get me a drink. "Ten minutes," he said as he put it down in front of me.

He was as good as his word. It was just ten minutes, and I

had finished my drink when he came up the other side of the bar and motioned to me.

"Let's go," he said.

We walked out the front door and stopped for our eyes to adjust to the sun. I noticed that Whitey was still parked across the street.

"Wait here for me for a minute," I said.

I walked across the street and straight up to his car. He ignored me until I was within two feet of him. Then he turned and stared at me out of those milk-blue eyes.

"Hello, Whitey," I said.

"Hello, March." There was a hint of a smile around his lips. "Looking for me?"

"Not exactly, but you're here and I could hardly miss you."

He shrugged. "What do you want, March?"

"Nothing. I just thought I'd come over and save you some work."

"Going to commit suicide?" he asked. I could see that he thought that was very funny.

"Not just yet. But I thought I'd tell you I'm going to spend the afternoon and early evening just relaxing. Then, at eleven tonight, I'm taking a plane to New York. I already have the reservation, and you can check it. It'll save you from following me around."

"I'm not working that hard," he said.

"No. Seems to me you were pretty busy while I was out of town."

"What does that mean?"

"Joe Capo."

"Oh, yeah, Joe. I was sorry to hear about him. A nice guy, but once in a while he gets in over his head. Too bad."

"I thought you'd feel that way," I said with a smile. "Well, I'll see you around, Whitey—I expect." I turned to cross the street.

"March," he said softly. I looked back at him. "You'll see me."

ELEVEN

During the afternoon, I phone the car rental agency and told them they could pick up the car at the airport. I stayed with Bo until about an hour after he went to work.

Then I went to the hotel, packed, and drove to International Airport. I picked up my ticket and had a leisurely dinner in the restaurant in the terminal building. I bought a magazine at the newsstand and retired to the bar until boarding time.

After the big jet was in the air, I opened the magazine and read until I began to get sleepy. Then I put out my cigarette, turned off the light, and went to sleep.

I was awake shortly before we reached Kennedy Airport. It was already daylight, and far below, New York City sprawled like an overweight harlot. I had time for a cigarette while we flew in a pattern over the field; then we went in for the landing.

I claimed my luggage and was going to get a taxi when I spotted a familiar figure over by one of the counters. It was Whitey Smith. He must have checked my reservation and then taken an earlier plane. I had company again.

The taxi let me out in front of my apartment on Perry Street, and I went up. It looked the same as it had when I left, but I had to throw open a window to clear out the mustiness. I took a quick shower, shaved, and put on a robe. I made myself some breakfast. Then I got dressed and went downstairs to get a cab. I told the driver to take me to the Intercontinental Building on Madison.

The girl at the reception desk looked up and smiled at me. "Hello, Mr. March."

"Hi, honey," I said. "Have you changed your mind about that luncheon date yet?"

"No," she said. "I'll tell Mr. Raymond's secretary you're here."

"You have a disagreeable way of being efficient," I said sourly.

She laughed and picked up the phone. A moment later she told me to go on back. I went through the door on the left and walked down to Martin's office. His secretary looked up from her desk.

"Home is the warrior," she said. "I don't know how you do it, buster, but you certainly manage."

"What does that mean?"

"I've got another voucher for money for you. And your ticket to Lisbon. You can pick them up on the way out."

"Okay," I said. I sat on the edge of her desk. "How's dear old Throcky getting along while I'm out of town?"

"Throcky?" she asked blankly.

"Our beloved president," I said gravely. "I met a classmate of his, and that's what he was called in college."

"Throcky! Oh, no!" She burst out laughing.

Just then the door to the office opened and Martin Raymond looked out. "Isn't he here—" He broke off as he caught sight of me. "Oh, there you are, Milo. Come on in."

I entered the office. Martin closed the door and held out his hand. "Milo, my boy. It's good to see you." He made it sound as if I'd been away for several years. "Can I give you a drink?"

"I thought you'd never ask."

He went over to his camouflaged bar and started pouring me a drink. That was a switch, too. Usually he told me to help myself, but this was the first time he'd ever served me.

"What was all the laughter about?" he asked as he handed me the drink.

"I just asked her how dear old Throcky was."

"Who's Throcky?"

"I'm surprised at you, Martin. He's our president."

A smile was tugging at his mouth, but he suppressed it. "Where'd you get that name?"

"I ran into one of his old college classmates."

"Well," he said, "I'd be careful about using it around here, if I were you. ... Now, tell me about the case."

I gave him a quick rundown on what I'd learned, leaving out a few things I thought were better kept to myself for the time being. "So," I concluded, "I have picked up a few things that nobody else knows at the moment. Sooner or later the FBI will get the same information. The plastic surgeon is a little scatterbrained, but he's liable to see one of the pictures of Crown and realize that this was his patient. In the meantime, however, I have a slight jump on everybody else, but I don't know how long it'll stay that way."

"You're doing a good job, Milo," he said. "I knew you would do it. We had a board meeting yesterday, and I want you to know that we're all proud of you."

"That's nice," I said dryly.

"The voucher is already made out for you to pick up more expense money and your ticket to Lisbon."

"I told you it would be expensive," I said. "Some of the information I've been getting had to be paid for, and I will undoubtedly have to pay for more."

"Think nothing of it," he said grandly. That attitude wouldn't last long. "What do you expect to find in Lisbon?"

"Where he went from there."

"How do you know he went somewhere else?"

"It's part of the pattern. I don't know how he acquired it, but this time Eugene Crown is showing the cunning of a fox. He hasn't left a clear trail and he isn't going to leave one."

"Well," Martin said loftily, "you'll find it."

"Maybe I should raise my fee to four hundred dollars a day."

That brought him back to reality. He frowned as if he were giving it serious thought. "I really don't think we can do that," he said with just the right tone of regret. "But if you clear this thing up, I think I can promise you a substantial bonus."

"You're playing my song," I told him. "Anything else on what we laughingly call your mind? I have things to do."

"Go ahead, my boy. And good luck." And he shook hands with me again. I decided I'd be glad when everything got back to normal.

"I'll see you," I said. I went outside and his secretary gave me the voucher and the ticket. I looked at the voucher. It was for five thousand dollars.

"Is that all?" I said. "Well, I guess I'll have to pinch every penny."

"Oh, boy," she said. "Now, I've heard everything. Be careful, or I may write a report on your penny-pinching for Throcky." She started to laugh again.

"Watch it, baby." I motioned toward the office door. "He doesn't think the help should have such a jocular attitude toward the head of the company—especially when we're engaged in a great public service. I'll see you around—and I'll think of you with every dollar I spend."

I went on down to the cashier and picked up my fifty $100 bills. The cashier looked as pained as if she were handing out her own money.

"Thanks, honey," I said, putting the money in my pocket. "I needed that. I have to take someone out for cocktails." I left while she was thinking about that.

The first thing I did was to put about half the money I had into American Express traveler's checks, which were accepted in almost every foreign country. The rest of the money I kept in cash. Dollars would come in handy when I had to buy any information.

Then I went to make certain that all my various shots were still good. They were, and I had the doctor give me a statement so I wouldn't have trouble getting into any country. Then I shopped for some clothes I might need on the trip and went downtown for lunch at the Blue Mill. After lunch, I picked up a couple of news magazines and two New York papers and went to my apartment. The first thing I did was put in a phone call to Larry Evans on the *Cleveland Press*.

"Hello, Larry," I said when he answered. "This is Milo March."

"Hi," he said. "Don't tell me you've solved the case already?"

"Not quite. I'm curious about something, and I thought you might be able to give me something on it."

"What?"

"That sterling citizen of Cleveland, Joe Capo. Somebody took a few shots at him the other night in Los Angeles."

"I know," he said. "It came over the wire service. What did you want to know?"

"He had to go somewhere to lick his wounds. I want to know if he came home or did he go somewhere else."

"Can I call you back?"

"Yeah." I gave him my home phone number. "Call me collect. I'll be here all afternoon and probably all evening, after I have dinner out. But I'm leaving New York in the morning."

"Where are you going?"

"No comment."

He laughed. "Okay. I should be able to call you back within an hour or so."

"I'll be here."

I hung up and made myself a drink, then started in on the papers and the magazines. Both magazines had follow-up stories on Crown, but they were only a rehash of the original story with some speculation about where he might be. They also mentioned Intercontinental's ad but treated it for laughs. I didn't blame them.

I made another drink and started reading the rest of the magazines and papers. A little less than two hours had gone by when the phone rang. It was the collect call from Larry Evans.

"Now you've got me curious," he said when I had accepted the call. "Joe Capo seems to have disappeared. He hasn't been seen in Cleveland since about two weeks ago. He hasn't been seen in Los Angeles since the night he was shot. I have a couple of pretty good informants, and they have no idea where he is."

"I expected that," I said. "I think he's gone into hiding, but was hoping I could get a lead on where he might go. But right now he's probably scared. I'm almost certain it was one of his co-workers who tried to kill him. That sort of thing can shake a man up."

"You mean the shooting was connected with the Randolph killing and Crown's disappearance?"

"That's exactly what I mean, but don't print anything about it yet. I don't want anyone to find out that I know even that much. I'll let you know when you can print something and give you more story."

"Okay," he said. "If I pick up anything, where can I reach you?"

"I don't know," I said truthfully. "Put in a collect call for me at this number. It'll be picked up by my answering service, and I'll eventually be in touch with them and then call you."

"All right. Good luck."

When I'd hung up, I called my answering service. There were no messages. I had another drink and read until it was time to go to dinner. I went to the Blue Mill for a steak, picked up the morning papers, and went back to the apartment. I packed my things for the next day, putting the gun and holster underneath the false bottom, then watched television until it was time to go to bed.

As the plane came in for the landing in Lisbon, I looked out the window at the candy-colored houses on the edge of the city. It was a pretty sight. I thought of the times I had been there before and remembered that there were a lot of sights in the city which were not so pretty, but they were hard to find unless you knew where to look.

It didn't take too long to go through Customs. My Portuguese is not great, but they understood Spanish, so we managed to communicate. I went out to get a taxi, trying to imagine how Eugene Crown would think when he first arrived in Lisbon.

"Take me to the best hotel in town," I told the taxi driver in Spanish. I knew a couple of the hotels, but I thought that would have been the way Crown would have found a hotel.

"*Si, Senhor,*" the driver answered.

After a short ride, we pulled up in front of a big, modern hotel. I had seen it before but had not stayed there.

I translated the charge for the ride into American money and gave him a dollar and told him to keep the change. I was overtipping him, and I was also sure he'd get rid of the dollar at a black market price and so have a bigger profit.

He thanked me profusely, and as I got out of the cab, I made sure to get the number of his cab. I went into the hotel to register. The clerk spoke Portuguese, Spanish, and English, so I decided to stick to the last.

"You will be staying long, Senhor March?" he asked.

"I don't know," I said. "It will depend on my business. Where can I go to change some dollars into local currency?"

"How much do you want?"

"I guess a hundred dollars to start with."

"We can do it for you, Senhor."

"Thank you," I said. I took out a hundred dollars and put it on the desk. He took it and went into the office. He came back and gave me a stack of Portuguese bills. I stuffed them in my pocket.

"By the way," I said, "a friend of mine was recently in Lisbon. I wonder if he stayed here? His name was Copper, Lance Copper."

"Senhor Copper? Yes, he was here. He left only two weeks ago."

"Went back to the United States, eh?"

"I do not know where he went. He did not say."

"Well, it's not important." I started to turn away to where the bellboy was waiting with my luggage and the key to my room.

"Senhor," the clerk said. He sounded hesitant. I turned to look at him. The expression on his face also indicated that he didn't know whether to speak or not.

"Yes?" I said.

"This Senhor Copper. He is a good friend of yours?"

"Not exactly. I know him fairly well, but he's more like a business friend. Why?"

"Well—" He hesitated and then plunged ahead. "I thought you might want to warn him if he comes to Lisbon again. For his own good. You understand?"

"I think so. What did he do? Get interested in women that he shouldn't have?"

"No, nothing like that. But he was friendly with a man who is not one of our better citizens. One who interests the police very much. It could make trouble for him."

"Oh," I said. "What sort of a man?"

"His name is Manuel Diaz. He is a *puto*. You know that word?"

"I know it," I said. It meant a male whore or pimp.

"He is not only that, he is a known thief. The police have arrested him many times. He came here to the hotel to see your friend many times, and they would leave together. It is a wonder that the police did not ask your friend about this."

"I understand. My friend is not wise in the ways of such things. I will speak to him when I see him. It is very kind of you to tell me, and I thank you."

He looked relieved. "It was the only thing to do. We try to take care of our guests."

"I see that you do. I shall remember it." I turned and followed the bellboy to the elevator and upstairs to my room. I tipped him and he left.

It was a large, comfortable-looking room, with a balcony from which it was possible to see the ocean. I unpacked my clothes and put them away. I lit a cigarette and stretched out on the bed for a minute. I was tired from the trip, and I knew there was little I could do until the following day.

The conversation with the clerk, I thought, had probably been a stroke of luck. It might give me a lead to where Crown had gone in Lisbon and what he'd done. On the other hand, however, it might turn out that it wouldn't lead me to anything but a broad.

Finally I got up and washed. Then I went downstairs. A bellboy pointed out the bar to me, and I went in. It was a large, pleasant bar. The sign back of it announced that the bartender spoke English. There were three men at the bar who looked like tourists. I sat some distance from them.

When the bartender came over I decided to take a chance. I had intended to play it safe and order Portuguese brandy. Instead I asked him for a very dry martini.

He served it and I took a taste. It was excellent. I saw that he was watching me, so I smiled and nodded. I went back to thinking about Eugene Crown.

I felt almost certain that he had come to Lisbon for one reason only—to get another passport. Herman Po had provided me with the name of a man who would supply it, but I didn't have his address. Of course, Crown might have used someone else. I remembered that one time I'd followed another man who had come to Lisbon for a passport and that then there had been several persons who specialized in passports.*

If Crown was doing what I thought he was, it was actually a pretty clever plan.

He undoubtedly knew that not only would the police be looking for him but that there would be others such as Whitey Smith. I doubted if anyone would have learned that he had come to Lisbon. I wouldn't have learned it, I expected, if it hadn't been for Herman Po. The question now was whether

---

* See *The Man Inside* by M.E. Chaber.

I could trace the next leg of his journey and his ultimate destination.

I ordered another martini. It had already occurred to me that Crown would probably try to end up in a country which had no extradition treaty with the United States. That limited the places he could go, which would make it a little easier. But not much. Such a country would make him fairly safe from the FBI. It wouldn't be much protection from the gunmen.

"Hello, March," a familiar voice said next to me. I turned to look. It was Whitey Smith.

"Hello, Whitey," I said wearily. I hadn't spotted him following me, but here he was. "You do get around, don't you?"

"So do you," he said. "What are you doing here?"

"On vacation. I haven't had one in a long time, and I decided I've been working too hard."

"Sure. Is that why you're not carrying your gun?"

"I'm not carrying a gun for the same reason you're not. These countries take a dim view of gun-toting Yankees, and they're pretty rough about it when they catch one. What are you doing in Lisbon?"

"I thought I needed a vacation too," he said with a humorless smile.

"I had an idea that you'd be busy trying to find Joe Capo. It must disturb you to leave unfinished business lying around."

He shrugged. "Joe's always around. I can find him if I want to. But why should I?"

"I heard that Joe has vanished since he was shot the other night."

"Maybe." He looked at me directly. "You think you know where that Crown guy is, don't you?"

I laughed. "So that's why you're following me around? Well, I haven't lost anyone named Crown. Have you?"

"I never lose anybody—unless I want to."

"Well, it's been very interesting talking to you—I think." I finished my drink. "I'll see you around, Whitey."

"You will."

I went into the dining room and had something to eat. Then I went into the lobby and looked at the newspapers. They had one in Spanish. I bought it and went to my room. It was late, but I relaxed and read the paper. There wasn't much in it. Then I went to sleep.

I was up early the following morning. I shaved, showered, and got dressed. I went downstairs and had breakfast. The coffee was good enough so that I had two cups before I went back to the lobby. There was a different clerk on duty behind the desk. This one didn't speak Spanish, but he did speak English. I asked him if he would get me a taxi.

He suggested that the doorman could get me one by merely raising his arm. I explained that I didn't want just any taxi but a special one. I told him the name and the number of the taxi I'd taken from the airport the night before.

"Ah," he said. "That is an independent taxi. It is the only taxi that man has."

"Can you get it for me?"

"I will try, Senhor." He got on the phone and soon was talking Portuguese so fast that I could only get part of it. Finally he hung up. "He will be here in a matter of moments.

Make yourself comfortable. The doorman will let you know when he is here."

I thanked him and went over to one of the chairs in the lobby. I lit a cigarette and picked up a magazine that was on a table. It was in Portuguese, but it consisted mostly of pictures, so I didn't bother about the text.

It wasn't long before the doorman appeared and called my name. I went out and got into the cab. The driver looked as if I'd gotten him out of bed. I probably had.

"Where do you wish to go, Senhor?" he asked as he pulled away from the curb.

That was the beginning of an interesting lesson in languages. He spoke Portuguese, which I partly understood but couldn't speak well; I was using Spanish, which he couldn't speak but understood.

"I do not know," I said.

He slowed down and looked back at me. "What?"

"Do you know a man named Manuel Diaz?" I asked.

"Senhor, there are many men in Lisbon named Manuel Diaz."

"I doubt if they are all like this one. He is a man of many interests, from women to the property of others, all of which are frowned upon by the officials."

"Oh, *that* Manuel Diaz. What about him, Senhor?"

"Do you know where to find him?"

"I think so, Senhor."

"I want to talk to him."

He shrugged, but the taxi picked up speed again. He drove about fifteen blocks, then pulled to the curb in front of a small café. "I will see if he's there, Senhor," he said. He slid out of the car and went into the café. A few minutes later he was back and climbed into the front seat.

"He is there. I told him you were one who wished to see him. He said he would consent to let you buy him a drink." He hesitated a minute. "He is a pig, that one, Senhor."

"I know," I said. "But when one wants ham, it is necessary to go to a pig. Where do I find him?"

"Inside, at a table to the right as you enter. You cannot miss him. He looks like a rat."

"All right," I said. I took out money and paid him, giving him a big tip. "When I want a taxi, I will always call you."

He nodded, smiling as he saw the size of the tip. I got out and entered the café, looking around as I stepped through the doorway.

The driver had been right. There was no mistaking him. He did look like a rat. He was small, with a pointed, very dark face. He had a thin mustache which made him look even more like a rat. I walked over to the table. He was picking his teeth with a sharp knife and didn't stop as he looked up at me.

"Senhor Diaz?" I asked.

"*Sim.*"

"I am Senhor March," I said in Spanish. "I would like to talk to you. May I buy you a drink?"

"*Sí,*" he said, switching to that language. He looked over at the bar and raised his voice to order his drink. Then he looked at me questioningly.

I raised my own voice and ordered a glass of Portuguese brandy. I sat down across from him. The bartender brought over the two drinks, and I paid him.

"A few weeks ago," I said when the bartender was gone, "a man came here from my country. His name was Lance Copper. He wanted to buy something, and he talked to you about it."

"So?"

"Who did you take him to? Rafael Garcias?"

He suddenly sat up, a look of astonishment on his face. He put the knife on the table. "You know Rafael?"

"No. I know of him, and I know someone who knows him."

"You also wish to buy something?"

I shook my head. "I only want to talk to Rafael Garcias. I know his name, but I do not know where to find him."

His face took on a hungry look. "You will pay?"

"Yes. Fifty dollars—in American money."

"It is not enough."

"It is all I will pay."

"But you do not know where to find him," he said triumphantly.

"There are dozens of ways to find where he lives," I said. "I am offering to pay you the fifty dollars because it will save me enough time to be worth it."

"You drive a hard bargain, Senhor," he said sullenly. "All right. Give me the fifty dollars and I will show you where he lives."

I shook my head. "I will give you half now and the other half when you show me."

He wasn't happy about it, but he held out his hand. I pulled a few American bills from my pocket and counted out twenty-five dollars and gave it to him.

"Where do we go?"

"Come," he said, standing up. "I will take you there. It is within walking distance from here."

I followed him out on the street. We turned to the right and walked along. Soon we came to a section that I remembered from another visit to Lisbon. On each side of the street there were little shops, below the level of the street, with what seemed to be living quarters above them. The shops had faded signs, and the windows were opaque with dirt.

"Here it is," he said, stopping.

I glanced at the shop next to us. A sign, which was barely legible, announced that spirits and works of art were for sale inside. Finally I could make out the name at the bottom of the sign. It was Rafael Garcias.

"For an additional twenty-five dollars," Diaz said, "I will go in with you and introduce you."

"I'll introduce myself," I said curtly. I gave him the rest of his money. "If I have further need of you, I will come to the café to find you."

He nodded, frowning, and walked away. I waited until he had gone a block, then I went down the steps and entered the shop. A bell tinkled as I opened the door.

I was in a medium-size room filled with small tables and chairs. In one corner there was a tiny counter, just large enough for one person to stand behind. Back of it there were shelves with bottles and glasses. Some of the bottles were covered with dust, as if they had been there, untouched, for years. They probably had. Apparently there was a room beyond that, for there was a curtained doorway.

I waited, and in a moment the curtains parted and a brisk little man entered. His hair was completely white, as was his fierce-looking mustache. He was obviously old, but his face was still young and so was his walk.

"Forgive me, Senhor," he said in English.

"It is nothing. Do you have Portuguese brandy?"

"*Sim.*"

"May I have a glass? Will you permit me to invite you to have a drink with me?"

"It will be an honor, Senhor." He went back of the counter and poured a glass of brandy. It was a generous portion. I noticed that he poured port for himself. He brought both glasses over to the table. I paid him, and he brought change from a drawer in the counter.

"I am called Milo March," I told him. "You are Senhor Rafael Garcias?"

"*Sim.*"

"It is you I have come to see. I was given your name by George Manning in the United States. He said that you are a great artist." Manning was the man in San Francisco who also made passports.

"The Senhor Manning is most kind. I have heard of him for years but have never met him."

I raised my glass in a toast to him and took a drink. It was good brandy.

"Sometime in the last few weeks a man from my country came to see you. When he arrived here, he was known as Lance Copper. I think that when he left it was with a new name. It is this that I wish to discuss with you."

His eyes were bright as he looked at me. "You are the police, Senhor?"

"No. The police of my country are looking for the man. So are some other men who want to kill him. I am hoping to find him before either of them do. I think it might save his life."

He nodded and took another taste of the port. "You do not want to buy the same thing he did?"

"No. I want to ask you three questions. But I am willing to pay for the answers to them. I will give you five hundred dollars in American money, which should be worth more on the black market. I am aware that a man must live."

"It is true. Tell me, Senhor, if you are not of the police, why are you doing this?"

"I work for an insurance company. They have become interested in the reason the police are looking for this young man. They have instructed me to find out why and how far he is involved in a case which is widely known in my country and because of which the two groups are looking for him. And to find him before they do."

"What are your three questions, Senhor? Tell me what they are, and then I will decide. If I tell you that I will not answer them, you owe me nothing."

"I want to know what name he is now using. Then, what kind of passport is he carrying. And, last, where did he go when he left Lisbon?"

He sipped at his port and stared off in the distance, thinking. Finally he looked at me again. "My decision must be based on whether I think you have spoken truthfully to me or not. I do not feel in my heart that you have been dishonest, so I will answer the three questions. He is using the name of Fane Hammer. He is carrying a West German passport which shows him to be a citizen of that country. When he left here, he was going to Hong Kong."

I counted out five hundred dollars and gave it to him.

I picked up my drink and finished it. "Senhor Garcias, I am eternally in your debt. If there is ever anything I can do for you, please call on me at once."

He smiled. "It is doubtful that I will ever be in your United States. When I was younger I might have looked forward to it, but now I am an old man and do not like to go as far as the store. But I thank you for the offer."

I shook hands with him, thanked him again, and left. It was a nice day, and I walked back to the hotel. When I reached there, I went straight up to my room. I put in a call to the air terminal and made a reservation for the flight to Hong Kong. Then I went downstairs and into the bar. I saw Whitey sitting in the lobby. A moment later he followed me and took the stool next to me. He ordered a drink and waited until it had been served.

"Have a good morning, March?" he asked.

"It was all right."

He took a drink from his glass and then looked at me with a smile. "Make your reservation for Hong Kong yet?"

TWELVE

That time he shook me up. I had known he'd be following me, but I didn't think he'd know where I was going almost as soon as I knew. There hadn't been any sign of him when I left the hotel in the morning. I'd have to be more careful about him in the future. I lit a cigarette and took a drink from my martini to give myself time to think.

"Yeah," I said, looking at him. "I was going to tell you to make one. I'd hate to lose you."

"You won't, March. I already have my reservation. I made it an hour ago."

"How'd you manage that?" I asked casually. "I just made mine."

"I knew you were going to make it," he said. He was obviously pleased with himself. "You wasted a lot of time, March."

"What does that mean?"

"I came down this morning and found you'd already left. I got the number of the taxi you'd taken and called the same one. I had the driver take me to the same place he'd taken you. And for a little extra he told me who you met there."

"So I guess you also met Manuel Diaz?"

"Yeah. That's where you wasted time. By being cheap. If you'd given him more money, he could've told you the only thing you needed to know. The next stop is Hong Kong. So I came back and made a reservation. Nothing to it."

"You should have made one for me while you were at it. I didn't realize that Manuel knew that much, or I might have offered him more. But it didn't really matter."

"Do you think Hong Kong is the end of the road?"

"For what?"

"Don't get cute with me, March," he said. "We both know what we're talking about. Eugene Crown. The pigeon."

"You really think you're going to catch up with him?" I asked.

"I'll catch up with him. I like it better when they run."

"I'll be there," I said quietly.

"I know." There was no expression in the milk-blue eyes as he glanced at me. "That's part of the fun. I looked you up, March. You knocked off a lot of good guys. It'll be a pleasure to even the score a little."

I finished my martini and motioned to the bartender for another one. He brought it over, and I took a sip before I looked at Whitey Smith.

"Be my guest, Whitey," I said evenly. "Anytime. Some of those good guys you were talking about had the same idea. You ought to check it out with some of them."

"I have. I visited one of them in the bucket. He's in a wheel-chair. Those kneecaps never did heal right. I made him a promise."

"That was sweet of you. Old pals and that sort of stuff? Too bad you won't keep it."

"I'll keep it. I always get what I go after."

"Like Joe Capo?"

"That's just delayed because you're on top of the list. I'll get back to him afterwards."

"Which way do you want to go? In a wheelchair like your friend? Or stretched out in a box? You guys are all alike. If you weren't shooting at guys who are scared, you'd never be able to hit anybody."

"You're not scared, March?"

"Of you?" I finished my drink. "Don't push too much, Whitey. I might not wait until you're ready." I got up and walked out.

There was nothing I had to do until the time the plane left the next day, so I decided to make like a tourist. I walked around the city looking at the buildings, went down to the ocean to see the fishing boats, and finally picked a small restaurant there to have a late lunch. It was worth it.

Later I just walked around, thinking about the case. In a way I was glad that Crown had gone to Hong Kong. I was certain that he had no intention of staying there, and I had two good contacts in that city. I could easily get information, and if I needed help to throw Whitey off, it would be available. I was glad for another reason. It would give me the chance of seeing Mei Hsu again. She was a Chinese woman I had known for a few years and the nearest thing to a special woman I had ever met. The only trouble was that she was too rich.*

I had dinner at a restaurant where I could get suckling pig. It was years since I'd had it, but it was worth the effort. After dinner I went to one of the cafés where I could hear Portuguese folk songs. They are sad but wonderful.

---

* See *Jade for a Lady* by M.E. Chaber.

It was late when I returned to the hotel. Whitey wasn't anywhere in sight. I had one more brandy at the bar and then went up to my room and went to bed, after leaving a wake-up call for the morning. The last thing I was aware of before I went to sleep was that I had to make certain that I reached Crown before Whitey did. If I didn't, the real answers to the death of Randolph would never be found.

I saw Whitey get on the plane the next morning shortly after I did. I paid no attention to where he was seated. I wanted him to continue to feel that there was nothing I could, or would, do.

It's a long flight from Lisbon to Hong Kong. I slept and drank and ate and slept and drank and ate. I don't get any special pleasure out of flying; it's merely convenient and saves a lot of time. So I just put up with it. I already knew what I would do when I reached there, so I retreated into a semiconscious state and endured.

As all things must, the flight finally came to an end. We glided down over the mountains and came to a stop on one of the runways. I went through customs and took a ferry to Hong Kong itself. There I got a taxi to take me to the American Hotel. I didn't even bother to see if Whitey was following.

I checked into the hotel and called room service to send up some ice and a bottle of V.O. I unpacked while I waited for the waiter to bring it.

I made myself a drink and sat down at the phone. I got out my little black book and put in a call. It was answered by a male voice, speaking Mandarin, announcing that I had reached the Hsu residence.

"Please tell Mei Hsu," I said in the same language, "that a friend from America is calling."

A moment later I heard her voice. "Milo, is that really you?"

"I think so," I said carefully. "I'm not really sure. Are you married yet?"

"I am waiting for you to ask me."

"I'd ask you," I said, "if you weren't so filthy rich. Think how it would feel if I had to come in every morning and ask you for a couple of pieces of old jade to pay off a poker debt from the night before."

"If it were Chinese poker, it would be all right. Where are you?"

"Hong Kong."

"When did you get in?"

"About fifteen minutes ago."

"What took you so long to call me? Want to come to the house for dinner?"

"You see how you are?" I said plaintively. "I call to ask you to have dinner with me, and before I can get it out you are inviting me to dinner. What time?"

She laughed. "About eight. I'll cook for you myself so you won't be reminded that I'm rich. I'll see you at eight. And … Milo …"

"Yes?"

"I'm so glad you're here. I can hardly wait until eight."

"I'll be there, honey."

I hung up and looked for another number. I called it. This time a voice answered in Cantonese and announced that I had reached the House of Po.

"Please inform Po Hing that March *hsien* wishes to speak with him."

There was a moment of waiting, then he came on the phone. "Milo," he said in English, "it's groovy to hear from you. Where are you?"

"Hong Kong. I just got in. I don't know how long I'll be here, and I want to see you for a few minutes. And I have a date tonight, which complicates it."

"The Hong Kong Dragon Lady, eh?" That was his name for Mei Hsu because after her father's death she had put together a gang of men to steal national treasure from the Chinese mainland.

"Yeah," I said.

"Why don't you marry the chick? She's loaded—don't bother to tell me that it's none of my business. Come on over. I'll have Wing Chok mix a fresh batch of martinis."

"I'll be there," I said. I hung up and started at once. I took the special elevator that was for swimmers and went out a side door from the basement. I walked around the pool and finally ended up on the street. I found a taxi and told him where I wanted to go.

Po Hing lived up in the hills, in a house that had cost a lot of money. He was the head of a gang that specialized in robbing ships that came into the harbor. He had never been caught. He was also useful to have as a friend. I rang the bell, and the door was opened by Wing Chok. He was unusually tall for a Chinese and was about as harmless as a cobra. He smiled at the sight of me.

"Welcome, March *hsien,*" he said. "He awaits you in his private room. You know the way."

"Yes," I said. "How are you, Wing Chok?"

"Well. We are busy, and much industry keeps one from illness. It has been said that only keeping busy makes a man forever happy."

"Careful. Don't let Po Hing hear you say that. You know he hates those old proverbs."

He laughed as I went on to the door that led into Po Hing's study. It was a huge room, filled with books and Oriental art; the only thing out of character was a modern desk—and Po Hing's suit, which was strictly Madison Avenue. Maybe the pitcher of martinis, too.

Po Hing waved from his chair behind the desk. I had never seen him except sitting in that chair. It was true he was a little on the chubby side, but he wasn't that fat.

"Greetings, cat," he said in English. He always talked like that to me. I suspected it was because he was barred from returning to San Francisco and he wanted to practice American lingo on me. "Pull up a chair and pour yourself a martini. You got here fast enough."

"It is written," I said in Mandarin Chinese, "that the truly thirsty man travels twice as fast as the man who lives on water." I poured a martini and added an olive from the bowl on his desk. "Old Chinese proverb—which I just made up. Your cousin Herman sent his regards."

"Herman is not just a square; he's a cube. How is he?"

"He seemed to be fine. And he's been a lot of help to me, so I dig him."

"You Occidentals are too scrutable," he said. "What are you doing in Hong Kong?"

"Working. What else? The one time I came here for a vacation, I was dragged back to work. They even called the fuzz on me."

"So you're working," he said. "That means you want something from poor old Hing."

"My heart bleeds for you," I said. "I came wanting two things from you. I wanted to look once again upon your cherubic, moonlike face and listen to the ancient Chinese wisdom pour from your lips. I also wanted to get some information—if you can find it for me."

"What do you mean—*if* I can find it?" he demanded indignantly. "Not a leaf stirs in Hong Kong without the knowledge of Po Hing. What do you want to learn?"

"About two weeks ago a man came here from Lisbon. He carried a West German passport, and according to it his name was Fane Hammer. I believe that Fane Hammer vanished shortly after he reached Hong Kong. I also believe that he bought another passport while he was here and then left for another destination. I want to know what kind of passport he bought and the name that's on it, and I want to know when he left Hong Kong and where he went."

"You don't want much, do you, chum? I can probably give you the answers you want. Will tomorrow be all right?"

"Tomorrow will be fine, Hing. But I don't want to put you out. I can always ask Mei Hsu to get it for me."

He glared at me. "What are you, some kind of nut? You think that dizzy broad knows more than Po Hing? She has a gang three times the size of mine, and she doesn't even make any profit. All she does is steal stuff from the mainland and put it away somewhere or sell some of the pieces and give the money to all those squares who come over her to get away from the Reds. She even has the nerve to call me when she's got a ship coming in and warn me not to touch it. Broads."

"I really got to you that time, didn't I?" I said with a smile. "Have you raided any of her ships?"

"No."

"Why not?"

"Well," he said with a sheepish expression on his face, "I don't dig all this ancestor jazz, but she just might have stumbled onto something. That's the trouble with dizzy broads. So why take a chance? I'd rather play a house game where I win no matter who else wins. This way I got a percentage play on both sides."

"Old sure-thing Po," I said, laughing. "You're a phony, Hing. Gold-plated. When you're an old man you'll probably go around quoting proverbs until everyone wants to strangle you."

He laughed. "You slay me, dad. Okay. I'll get the information for you. What did this cat do?"

"He's accused of having killed a man. Most people believe that he did. I'm not so sure about it. In the meantime the cops are looking for him—but so is a professional killer. If he is guilty of the assassination, why not let the cops take him and let him be executed?"

"Why didn't the hoods just kill him right away in the States?"

"He turned out to be smarter than they thought he was. He gave them the slip and disappeared."

"So you got the jump on the cops and the hoods?"

"For the most part. But one hood has managed to follow me. He's in Hong Kong now."

"You want somebody to hit him?"

"Thanks, Hing, but no. I think the hood is important to the case, so I'd rather have him alive. I'll shake him."

"I'll call you tomorrow. Where are you staying?"

"American Hotel."

"Okay. Have another martini and tell me about San Francisco."

Poor Hing. The one thing missing in his life was San Francisco. I never knew the reason why, but I gathered that the police there were anxious to talk to him. Anyway, I had another martini and told him as much about San Francisco as I could.

"Well," I said when I had run out of information, "I'd better run along. All right if I phone for a cab?"

"Don't bother, pal. Wing Chok will drive you back to the hotel." His hand reached beneath the desk and I knew he was pressing a button. A moment later the door opened and the big Chinese looked in. Hing told him to take me back, and he nodded.

"Thanks, Hing," I said.

He waved his hand. "I thank you. You sure brought back a lot of old memories. I miss that burg."

I went out with Wing Chok, and we drove to the hotel. He let me out in front of it. I went up to my room and checked the time. I decided I could devote a couple of hours to a nap. I called the operator and asked her to call me in two hours. I took off part of my clothing and stretched out on the bed.

The phone awakened me right on time. I shaved and showered and dressed, then went downstairs. I had a little time to kill, so I went into the bar. Whitey was in there having a drink. I went down and took a stool next to him. If I didn't, he'd only join me.

"Hello, Whitey. How do you like Hong Kong?"

"What's to like? It's just a big Chinatown. Where have you been?"

"Just now? Taking a nap. Incidentally, I'm going out in a few minutes. There's no point following me. I've got a date, and she doesn't have a sister."

"We'll see," he said. "Is this the end of the trail, or do we have to go somewhere else?"

I shrugged. "I don't know. I haven't asked. I'm going to enjoy myself for a couple of days. Then maybe I'll go to work." I ordered a dry martini from the bartender.

We didn't do any more talking, which was just fine with me. I finished my drink and went out. The doorman got a taxi for me. I gave the driver the address. As we pulled away from the curb, I looked back and saw Whitey getting into another taxi.

Mei Hsu lived in the hills above the city. It was a huge, beautiful house which had belonged to her father. I paid the driver and walked up to the front door without even looking back to see where Whitey was.

The door was opened by a young Chinese who smiled when I gave him my name. He told me to go right upstairs. Mei Hsu had remodeled the second floor, turning it into her private apartment. I knocked on the door, and she called for me to come in. I opened the door.

She was coming across the room toward me. I stopped where I was and just stared. She was wearing a brightly colored Chinese dress with the high-collar and the slit skirt.

"What's wrong, Milo?" she asked.

"Whenever I'm away from you, I forget how beautiful you are until I see you again. Then it hits me with the same impact as the first time I saw you."

"Then you shouldn't stay away so long." With that, she came into my arms with a little rush.

I held her tight for a couple of minutes, then kissed her. I meant it to be a short hello-kiss, but it turned into something else. It lasted until she finally put her hands on my chest and pushed me away. We were both a little breathless.

"Milo," she said, "if you keep that up, the martinis will get warm and the dinner will be ruined."

"To hell with both of them!"

She shook her head, laughing. "I've worked too hard to make it a good dinner. Besides, I just want to sit and look at you for a while. Do you like my dress?"

"On you, yes. But then you always look beautiful in anything—or out of it." I switched to Mandarin Chinese. "It is truly said that compared to you the lotus flower fades into a ragged weed."

"That is one of the things I love about you, Milo," she said. "You always think of the right thing to say and the right language to say it in. Come on." She took me by the hand and led me over to the couch. She held on to my hand after we sat down.

There was a low teakwood table in front of us. On it there

was a pitcher of martinis nestling in a bucket of crushed ice. There were two martini glasses, a dish of olives, and a plate of small Chinese pastries, which I knew were filled with meat and seafood.

"I asked you about the dress," she said, "because it's my happy dress and I'm wearing it because you're here. Pour our drinks."

I poured the martinis and added the olives. I lifted my glass. "To you, darling."

"I'd rather drink to us," she said. We clicked glasses and drank. "I suppose you're in Hong Kong on business again?"

"Yes."

"It would be nice if you came only to see me."

"If you'll remember, I did come here once on a vacation and was here about a day when the company dragged me back. They even pulled strings to get that British police inspector to threaten to have me kicked out as an undesirable."

"You should have called me as a witness. I would have told them that you are most desirable. What's the job this time?" She took one of the pastries and put it in my mouth.

"That," I said when I'd eaten it, "is just like a woman. Ask a question and then fill my mouth so I can't answer. You don't want to hear about it anyway."

"But I do. That's the only way I have of sharing part of your life."

I gave her a quick rundown on the case and why I was in Hong Kong. "After I talked to you," I concluded, "I saw Po Hing. He said he could get the information for me by tomorrow."

"Po Hing!" she said. "I can get the information for you easier and quicker."

"I didn't want to bother you with that."

"Nonsense," she said. She got up and went over to the phone and dialed a number. "What was the name of the man, the one he used in entering here?"

"Fane Hammer. He had a West German passport."

She turned back to the phone and began to talk rapidly in a dialect I couldn't understand. Finally she hung up and came back to the couch.

"We should have most of the answers by the time we finish dinner. What are you doing on this case, Milo? I thought you always worked on insurance cases."

So I explained why I was on it. I had already told it so many times, and I couldn't even believe it myself.

"I still don't understand why you're working on it," she said when I had finished.

"I don't either," I confessed. "The nearest I can come to it is that my company is determined to prove that a large corporation can have a soul and they're going to do it if it kills me. Which it won't. It is an interesting case, and I like the money."

"Money," she said with the scorn that always marks someone who has it. "Why don't you quit your job and let me put up enough money to go into some nice business? You could always pay back the investment."

I laughed. "For a minute I thought you were going to invite me to join your gang that's raiding the China mainland. That I might like. But I've been in this business too long. A nice business would bore me to death."

We had two more martinis and caught up with the things that had been happening since we'd last seen each other. Then we went in to dinner. As usual, when she cooked, it was superb.

"Look at you," I said when I couldn't eat any more. "You're beautiful, you're wonderful in the hay, and you're a marvelous cook. If you only didn't have so damn much money—"

"Maybe I could give part of it away," she suggested.

I shook my head. "It wouldn't work, honey. There would come a time when you'd resent that you'd done it because of me. And I'd probably still be known as Mr. Hsu."

The phone rang. She went to answer it and talked in the same dialect she had used before. Finally she hung up and came back. "Let's go in the other room," she said. "I'll bring some brandy."

"What about this?" I asked, indicating the table. "Want me to help you clean up?"

"No. The maid can do it tomorrow."

"You see," I said as I followed her into the other room.

She got a bottle of brandy and two glasses from a cabinet and poured out two drinks. "That was from one of my men. I have most of the information for you. Your man obtained a new passport from Chan Luk, who does good work. It was a Dutch passport in the name of Melford Pare. He also had Chan Luk forge some other papers for him for entry into South Africa."

"What part of South Africa?"

"I don't know. None of Chan Luk's work indicated the city. But I can find that easily enough early in the morning. I suppose that all I am accomplishing is helping you to leave Hong Kong sooner."

"I had already planned on being able to leave day after tomorrow. I have to move as fast as possible. I've got a lead on everyone else, but I can't expect to keep it forever."

"So I have tonight and tomorrow night?"

"That's about it, honey. I'm sorry. I'd like to be here longer."

"Well," she said, lifting her glass, "here's to tonight and tomorrow night."

There was no more talk about business. We sipped our brandy and talked about ourselves. Finally I put my glass down and kissed her again. We lost all interest in talking. I stood up and led her to the third room.

I was awake early the next morning. Mei was still asleep as I dressed quietly. I looked at her and blew her a silent kiss. I went into the living room and used the phone to call for a taxi. I wrote a short note for Mei and left the house without seeing anyone else. The taxi showed up shortly and took me back to the hotel.

When I reached my room, I called room service and ordered breakfast, any early newspapers, and a bucket of ice. I removed my jacket and tie and kicked off my shoes. It wasn't long before the waiter arrived with my order. I added the tip to the check and signed it. When he was gone I poured some V.O. over ice and sat down to contemplate the breakfast.

After I ate, I made another drink and stretched out on the bed with the newspapers. All I had to do was wait for phone calls.

The first one came at ten o'clock. It was Po Hing. He gave

me the same information Mei Hsu had gotten the night before. He promised to try to find out the one remaining fact I needed and hung up.

The phone rang again in about fifteen minutes. I picked it up and said hello.

"Good morning, darling," she said. "Why didn't you awaken me? It was terrible waking up and finding you gone."

"You looked so beautiful and peaceful, I didn't have the heart to bring you back into the world of reality. How are you?"

"I'm wonderful. Did you have any breakfast?"

"As soon as I got back to the hotel."

"And I was going to make your breakfast for you. … I have the rest of the information for you. Your Melford Pare left Hong Kong a week ago on his way to Cape Town."

"I thought that might, be where he'd go. Thanks, honey."

"What will we do today and tonight?"

"What time tonight?" I asked, and she laughed. "What would you like to do?"

"Will it be all right if I pick you up in about two hours?"

"Fine. Then what?"

"Milo, do you remember where we went for dinner on our first date?"

"Sure. To one of the floating restaurants."

"I thought it would be fun to drive out of the city and down in that direction. I know a little place where we can get a wonderful lunch. Then we can spend the afternoon just driving around, or maybe we'll go up in the hills and sit on the grass. We'll have dinner on the boat."

"That sounds great. I'll be ready in two hours. Just tell the doorman to look for me in the bar."

"I'll see you then, darling."

I shaved and showered and slowly got dressed. I finished reading the newspapers. There wasn't anything in them on my case, but at least I was keeping up with things. I packed my bag and then went downstairs. First, I went to see the doorman.

"My name is Milo March," I said, giving him some money. "Someone will drive up here before long and ask for me. I'll be in the bar."

"Yes, sir. Thank you, sir."

I went into the bar. Sure enough, Whitey was there. I went to sit next to him. I ordered a dry martini and didn't say anything to him.

"You stayed pretty late last night, March," he said.

"I always stay late," I said. "I told you I had a date and that I was going to enjoy myself for a couple of days. You ought to learn to believe people."

"Yeah?"

"As a matter of fact, the same lady is soon going to pick me up here. We're going to spend the afternoon out of the city and have dinner out of the city. Then we're going back to the same house where I went last night. I will not look kindly upon being followed all that time. Is that clear?"

"Yeah. I'll make my mind up later. I haven't seen the broad yet."

"Lady."

"Okay. We'll see."

"This time you'd better, baby. It would be a pity if I had to kill you before you found out where Crown is."

He gave me another of those milk-blue stares. "You know where he is?"

"No, but I won't leave until I do."

"Okay." He paused for a minute. "What the hell do you do in this town?"

"You know what I'm doing here," I said with a smile.

"Yeah. You know people. What do strangers do?"

"Just a minute and I'll get the answer for you." I got up and went to the public phone. I called Po Hing and asked him for the address of a whorehouse.

"For you?" he asked.

"No. For someone I don't like very much."

He laughed and gave me an address. "What's his name?"

"Whitey Smith, but he may not use his name. He's easily recognized. He's got snow-white hair, but he's not that old. And he's tall. About six two."

"Okay, pal. I own the joint. I'll see that he gets special treatment."

"Thanks, Hing."

"It's a pleasure, pal."

I went back to the bar and wrote down the address and put it in front of Whitey. "Try that place."

"Broads?"

"Broads. The best in town."

"Thanks, March," he said, putting the paper in his pocket. "We'll see."

I had almost finished my drink when the doorman appeared and called my name. I got up and left.

She had one surprise for me. The car parked in front was a Rolls-Royce. She had class, that girl. I started to get in, but she stopped me. "You drive," she said.

I went around and got behind the wheel. As I drove away, I glanced in the rearview mirror and saw Whitey standing on the sidewalk and watching us.

"Do you remember how to get there?" Mei asked.

"I'm not sure."

"I'll tell you the way. The place where we are having lunch doesn't serve drinks, so I brought along a thermos of martinis."

I glanced at her. "You think of everything, baby. I think we should get to know each other better."

"That's what I've been telling you," she said smugly.

We drove up into the hills and then followed a winding road that crossed them and finally made its way down to the water. We drove past the restaurant boats, continued for a few miles, and then stopped at a tiny place she indicated. We had a couple of martinis from the thermos jug and then went inside. She was right. The food was great.

Later we drove up into the hills, parked, and sat on the grass. From there we could see across to the mainland. It was hard to believe that we were that near to Red China.

When evening came, we got back in the car and drove down to where the restaurant boats were moored. We were rowed out to one of the boats. We walked around to tanks of fish and picked out the ones we wanted. It was a dinner very much like the one we'd had on our first date.

Afterwards we drove straight back to her house. There hadn't been any sign of Whitey, so I guessed he'd gone to the address I'd given him. I wondered what kind of special treatment Po Hing had provided for him.

It was almost ten o'clock when we reached the house. I waited until we were in the apartment and then asked her if I could use the phone to call New York City. It was a call that I hadn't wanted to make from the hotel because it was always possible Whitey had gotten to one of the operators. Mei told me to go ahead, and I put in a call for Martin Raymond. It went through speedily.

"Milo," he said, "where are you?"

"Hong Kong."

"What are you doing there?"

"The same thing I was doing in Lisbon and all over the United States. Look, this ain't a local call. I want to know something. Is there an insurance company in Cape Town, South Africa, that we do business with?"

"Yes. It's Cape Town Mutual, Limited. Why?"

"Do we have enough of a relationship that I could go to them if necessary and ask for some minor assistance without telling them what the case is?"

"I don't see why not. We underwrite a lot of their insurance. The only man I know there, from correspondence, is a Hendrik Du Plessis. What's up?"

"I'll tell you later."

"Is that where our man has gone?"

"I think so, but keep your mouth buttoned. Don't even talk in your sleep. I'll be in touch, Martin." I hung up on him.

I tried to pay Mei for the call, but she wouldn't let me. Finally I got tired of arguing with her.

"There are three other things I want," I told her. "I want to get up early in the morning, and I want somebody to either go with me to the hotel or meet me there. But first I want you to call the airport and see if you can make a reservation on a plane for Cape Town tomorrow. Make the reservation in any name, and I will go to the airport and be able to get the ticket when it isn't picked up."

She nodded and went to the phone. A moment later there was a reservation in the name of Guy Jones.

"Now," I said, "about the fellow who will meet me at the hotel or go there with me. I want him to take my luggage out of the hotel and check it into the air terminal in my name."

Again she went to the phone and in Cantonese repeated to someone what I had said. She hung up. "His name is Kwang Li. He will be waiting for you downstairs in the morning. He is reliable. What's the third thing?"

"I may be followed when I leave the hotel to go to the airport. If I am, he will be an American, over six feet tall, with completely white hair. He's probably no more than forty. The hair is cut quite close. I want him stopped and delayed long enough so that he can't follow me or can't reach the airport until after the plane has left."

"That is easy. Do you want him badly hurt?"

"Not necessarily. Just detained long enough. And remember one thing. He is a dangerous man. He has killed a lot of people."

"I will remember."

"Can you have me awakened early in the morning?"

"I will awaken you myself, darling."

It would be our last night together for some time, so it was very late before we went to sleep. But she awakened me at the right time, and when I came out of the shower, there was a drink, breakfast, and coffee waiting for me. While I ate, I asked her to phone for a taxi, but she said that Kwang Li had a car. I also asked her about paying Kwang Li, and she told me that he would be insulted.

Then it was time to go. I took her in my arms and kissed her.

"Please come back soon, Milo."

I switched to Chinese. "My feet will grow wings that it may be possible."

"And mine," she answered in the same language, "will be burdened with weights until you return."

With that I left. Kwang Li was waiting downstairs, and we drove straight to the hotel. I thought it unlikely that Whitey Smith would be around that early to see me coming in, but he might be there when I left. And even if he was detained, he'd be back to ask questions.

Kwang Li went with me into the hotel. I went straight to the desk and told the clerk I would be checking out within an hour or so but that I wanted to pay the bill at once. After paying it, I told him that Kwang Li would be taking my luggage with him and that I was going to visit a friend for a few days.

We went up to the room, picking up a newspaper on the way. I had Kwang Li wait until I shaved. Then I poured myself a drink and made sure that everything was packed, and sent Kwang Li on his way.

I sipped the drink and read the newspaper, frequently

glancing at my watch. Finally it was time to go. I went downstairs, and the doorman motioned one of the waiting taxis to move up. I got in and told the driver to go straight down the street and then I would tell him where to go. He pulled away from the curb.

I twisted around in the seat and looked through the rear window. Whitey Smith came running from the hotel and leaped into the next taxi in line without waiting for the doorman to get it for him. It pulled out to follow my taxi.

Before I could even accept what I saw, there was a loud crash and the screaming of torn metal.

THIRTEEN

Everything happened so fast it was difficult to grasp at once. There had been an old, scarred Jaguar parked just back of the taxis. It had pulled out, then with a sudden surge of power had leaped straight into the taxi in which Whitey was riding. The two drivers immediately leaped out and began screaming at each other in Chinese. Within a matter of seconds other Chinese appeared, joining the argument on one side or the other. There must have been at least twenty of them surrounding the taxi.

It must have been a frustrating situation for Whitey. He was sitting there surrounded by a screaming and shoving crowd, unable to understand what was being said, while he watched me getting farther away every second. He did what probably seemed a normal thing. He opened the taxi door and got out, obviously intending to get another cab. But there was no way through the seething wall of flesh. The Chinese had started to fight among themselves, and suddenly Whitey vanished from my sight, apparently hit by a wild blow. I thought it might not have been so wild at that.

I told my driver to take me to the ferry and relaxed. It looked like Mei Hsu was doing a good job. Just to be on the safe side, I glanced behind a few times, but there was nobody following. When we reached the ferry I went aboard and crossed over to the terminal.

There was no need to wait for the shadowy Mr. Jones not to show up. They didn't have a full load, so I picked up my ticket at once. I got my luggage from the checkroom and left it to be put aboard. I went to the bar to wait. From there I could see the main part of the terminal, and there was still no sign of Whitey by the time they announced the plane was loading. I joined the others at the gate.

It wasn't many minutes before the big jet lifted from the field and headed back toward the other side of the world. I unfastened my seat belt, lit a cigarette, and when the stewardess came along, ordered a drink. I was looking forward to the long flight with a lack of enthusiasm.

I spent much of the time sleeping. For the rest, I drank and ate or stared morosely out the window at nothing. Finally, as all dull things must, the flight also ended as the pilot announced that we were about to land at Cape Town. I came out of my stupor and looked through the window. That is one part of flying I like, looking down at a city. Each one has a separate personality when viewed from above. In looking at Cape Town I could see evidence of its variety, of its different peoples with their different situations. I thought, with irony, that one who was experienced in such city-reading would even be able to detect the existence of South Africa's apartheid.

It didn't take long to go through customs. Among other things, I stated that I was there for a vacation. When they'd finished, I took a taxi to the Mount Nelson Hotel. It was the only hotel name I knew. I registered and was taken to my room. It was a pleasant room with a view of the ocean. I unpacked, showered and shaved, and put on fresh clothes. Then I had valet service pick up a suit to be cleaned and some laundry.

Later, I went downstairs and tried the bar. There was a comfortable air about it. I had one drink and then went outside and looked around. There was a large lawn sloping away from the hotel, and I noticed there were several people sitting in chairs placed on it. I returned to the lobby and bought an English-language newspaper. I then found a hotel servant, a light-skinned black African, who got a chair and placed it on the lawn at a spot I indicated. I tipped him and sat down.

First, I looked around. I had a partial view of the gardens, which were beautiful, and directly in front of me a part of the town, which sloped down to the ocean. I realized, half-forgotten memories returning, that this was where the first Dutch settlers had landed. I leaned back and read the newspaper. There wasn't much in it.

Finally my mind, as though partly rested, came back to my more immediate problem. Where would Eugene Crown—especially the "new" Crown—go, and what would he do? Would he stay in Cape Town? I thought that the answer to that would be yes—at least temporarily. There was no way of knowing how much money he had left, or even how much he had started with, but it certainly wouldn't last forever. He'd have to find some way of earning money. That wouldn't be easy in a strange country, but it would be even more difficult for Crown because he had little education and no special skills.

There was another important question. Crown had spent slightly more than half his life committing crimes. I had a feeling that now he would try to lead a law-abiding existence, but would a lack of early success drive him back to crime in South Africa? It was difficult to answer. Having spent all his life feeling handicapped in that area, he'd probably be anxious to make up for lost time. I didn't know, but I had a suspicion that it might not be too easy to do in South Africa.

There was nothing in my thinking that gave a clue about where to start looking for him. I might have to depend on the local insurance company. They should be able to get access to some official sources which would be closed to me.

I got up and walked through the gardens toward what seemed as though it might be a business section. It was. After walking several blocks I came to a bank. I went in and exchanged some of my money for local currency.

Directly across from the bank there was a tobacco shop. I went over and asked about American cigarettes. The man told me he had some but that the price was rather higher than the others. I bought a carton, and he was right about the price. I went back to the hotel.

Having decided that I would wait until the next day to go to the insurance company, I spent the rest of the day and evening in the hotel. I had dinner in the dining room, and it was quite good. Then I picked up a few magazines and went to my room. I read until I went to sleep.

I awakened the next morning, feeling more rested than I had in several days. I had breakfast in my room, looked up the address of Cape Town Mutual, and took a taxi to the offices. I told a girl who I was and where I was from, and asked to see Mr. Du Plessis.

Before long I was shown into a large office. The man behind the desk stood up as I entered. He was a large man with a pleasant face and a well-fed look.

"Hello, Mr. March," he said, holding out his hand.

I shook hands with him, and we both sat down. I took out my identification and showed it to him. He examined it and handed it back. "We've been doing business with Intercontinental for years," he said, "but you're the first person from the company I've ever met. What brings you to Cape Town, Mr. March?"

"I'm looking for a man," I said. "An American who came to Cape Town within the last week. Mr. Raymond, one of our vice-presidents, suggested that you might be able to help me."

"I'm familiar with Mr. Raymond's name. We'll be happy to give you any assistance we can. I'll have one of our investigators come in." He picked up the phone and asked somebody to have Mr. Wilkins step in. He turned back to me with a smile. "A case you're working on, Mr. March?"

"Yes."

"I imagine you are aware that if you do locate your man, you may run into certain difficulties about having him extradited?"

"I know," I said, "but I'll worry about that when I reach it. I imagine that your office will be able to recommend a good attorney if I need one?"

"Certainly."

The door opened, and a blond young man came in. Du Plessis introduced us. The young man's name was Fred Wilkins. We shook hands.

"Fred," Du Plessis said to me, "is in my opinion the best insurance investigator in South Africa. If anyone can help you, he's the man." He turned to Wilkins. "Mr. March has a problem and would like an assist from us. I wonder if you'd take him along to your office and see if you can do anything for him." It was an order, not a question, and Wilkins and I both understood this.

"Certainly, sir," Wilkins said and looked at me.

I shook hands once more with Du Plessis and thanked him. Then I followed Wilkins out and to a simple, almost stark office. He sat down behind his desk, and I took the chair next to it. I saw there was an ashtray on his desk, so I offered him a cigarette and took one myself. I lit both of them.

"I take it," he said dryly, "that you are in the insurance business, Mr. March?"

"Milo," I said. I took out my identification and put it in front of him. "Intercontinental Insurance. My title is the same as yours."

He looked at the card and handed it back to me. He smiled for the first time. "I thought you might be a VIP since you were in the office of Mr. Du Plessis."

"I rather imagine that Du Plessis is playing it close to his chest," I said. I had deliberately left out the "Mister." "Intercontinental underwrites many of your policies, and I think he wanted to be careful until he was certain of how much weight I carry."

He chuckled. "That sounds about right." He gave me a

straight look, still smiling. "How much weight *do* you carry—Milo?"

I smiled back. "In the day-to-day decisions of the office, I have none. In any investigation on which I work, I have all the weight. I do what I think best, including the amount of their money I spend, and normally I make no report until the case is completed. There is, however, one thing that does have a bearing on this. I am not a salaried investigator. When I work it's on a per-diem-plus-expenses deal, and that is the only way I'll work for them. They do have first call on my services, but in between assignments I can work for someone else. But I'd say that ninety percent of my work is for Intercontinental."

"Sounds good. If there's ever another assignment like that, let me know. How can I help you, Milo?"

"A man arrived in Cape Town within the past week. He is an American, but he's traveling on a Dutch passport. His name is Melford Pare. I'm aware that as an American insurance investigator there isn't much I can do without having doors slammed in my face—and I bruise easily. I want to know where this man is staying at the moment. If possible, without putting you to too much work, I would like to know what he's been doing since he arrived here. Primarily, socially."

"The first I can do easily and quickly," he said. "I might be able to get the second easily, too. You see, social circles here are very circumscribed and not easy to surmount. Is he young?"

"Middle thirties."

"Interested in girls?"

"I would say decidedly so."

"That would be tough," he said. "A lot of entertaining, even just drinking, is done in private homes. If they know you for a long time they will invite you. If not, they won't. There are, of course, houses of prostitution. There are also nightclubs and bars, but usually people go to them in couples, and they're not places to pick up girls. He might have an easier time if he tried to move in colored circles, but that would do him harm if he also wanted to move in white circles."

"It sounds complicated."

"It is. There are four different social groups. There are the whites—who also include a few coloreds, what you might call mulattoes, who have been able to move in for one reason or another. There are the coloreds, which are mostly mixtures of white and black races, but it also includes Chinese—but not Japanese.* There are Indians. Then there are Bantus, which actually includes everyone with a black skin. It tends to make things difficult for outsiders such as the man you're looking for. But I'll see what I can dig up."

"Thanks. I'll appreciate it. I'm staying at the Mount Nelson, and I'll wait to hear from you."

"All right. Probably by tomorrow. Is this an insurance fraud case you're working on?"

"Not exactly," I said carefully. "Actually, I cannot tell you more than the fact that I am working for Intercontinental. Not yet. But I promise you that when it is finished I will tell you the whole story—or you will be able to read it in your newspapers."

* In 1984, Chinese were allowed the same privileges as Japanese under apartheid. The official end to this system of legalized racism came in 1994.

"Fair enough. I will phone you as soon as I have anything to report."

I thanked him again and went back to the hotel. On the way back, I stopped and bought a pair of slacks and a fairly quiet sport jacket. I decided that I wouldn't do anything until I heard from Wilkins, and there would be no need for me to wear a suit every minute of every day. I had stopped on the Strand, which was only a few blocks from the hotel, so I visited a store that had a large selection of magazines. I bought several and then walked to the Mount Nelson.

I spent the rest of the day in the hotel, reading and drinking and eating. After dinner, I stayed in my room reading. I had a nightcap from the bottle of V.O. and went to sleep.

The next morning I was up early, feeling I'd had enough sleep to last me a week. After I'd shaved and showered, I phoned down for breakfast and a bucket of ice. I had one drink and ate. The valet service brought back my suit and laundry. I went back to reading.

The phone rang shortly before noon. I picked up the receiver and said hello.

"Milo? This is Fred Wilkins. I'm down in the lobby, and I think I have some news for you."

"I'll be right down," I said. I shrugged into the new sport jacket and went out to the elevator.

I spotted Wilkins almost as soon as I stepped out of the elevator. I went over and shook hands with him. "Let's go into the bar," I said. "I'll buy you a drink."

As we entered, we passed a young man coming out. He looked vaguely familiar, but it wasn't until we were already on stools that I suddenly realized who it was. Eugene Crown—with the pulled-in ears and no scar.

We ordered drinks. He had a scotch and water, and I had a martini. He waited until the drinks had been served and paid for. Then he turned to me with a slight smile.

"First, I can tell you where Melford Pare is staying. Here in the Mount Nelson."

"I just guessed that," I said. "As we came in, we passed him going out."

"You know what he looks like?" he asked, covering his disappointment at not having surprised me.

"Yeah. I didn't realize that's who it was until we were already seated at the bar. He's had his features changed slightly, and I was still thinking of the way he originally looked."

"If you know what he looks like, you shouldn't have any trouble getting the police to pick him up. Of course, you'll have the problem of extradition."

"I know," I said unhappily. "Frankly, just between us, I'd rather try to get acquainted with him before he knows who I am, and it might be possible to talk him into going back voluntarily. I've been followed most of the way by a man who wants to kill him. If that fails, I might be able to arrange for him to be deported."

"On account of the passport? I guessed from something you said yesterday that it must be spurious."

"Again between you and me, it is. It's a Dutch passport, and I could get him extradited from there."

He nodded. "Well, here's the rest of it. He has a permit to

stay here to look for work. If he gets it, he would have no problem. If he doesn't, he might get it renewed for one more short period. Incidentally, he stated that his occupation was interior decorator."

I laughed. "In a way, that's true. He's decorated some of the best-known interiors in America. But I wouldn't think there was too big a call for that profession here."

"There is some, but it's hard to compete with the ones who are established. They usually have to be Afrikaans or English—preferably the former. Of course, the very rich bring them in from Paris or London. He is not necessarily limited to the stated occupation. If he can land another type of work, especially if it's one here that needs people, he'll be able to stay."

"I don't think that's much of a problem," I said. "Either I'll get him, or the man following me will. And he'll have to get me along with this man if he's to succeed."

"You're serious?" he asked.

"Deadly—if you'll forgive the pun. Anything else?" He'd finished his drink, so I motioned to the bartender for two more.

He waited until we had the drinks and the bartender had retreated. "I did some checking on the second part of your request, and I think I have about all that it's possible to get covering the short time he's been here. He obviously knows no one in Cape Town. He has been to two nightclubs, not far from here. He also was obviously there looking for girls and, of course, had no success."

"How did you find that out?"

"It was easy. In both places he introduced himself to the bartender and made it known he was looking for a girl. In both instances, the bartenders considered him pushy and a bit of a bounder. Both of the men were English, by the way. The Afrikaans would have used different expressions, more or less adding up to the same thing."

"I guessed that in advance. Didn't he try to make passes at any of the women who were escorted?"

"I gather not. It wouldn't have done him any good if he had. Oh, I don't say that there isn't adultery here. There's probably as much as anywhere. But they tend to be very quiet about it, much as they do in England. I often think it's one of the greatest influences that England has exerted on South Africa."

I laughed. "You're probably right. Why don't you stay and have lunch with me?"

"I'd enjoy that," he said simply.

We went into the dining room, where I ordered two drinks for us, and then we had lunch. We talked mostly about insurance. He told me a little about the sort of cases they had in Cape Town, and I told him of a couple of cases I'd worked on in the past. I walked out to the lobby with him afterwards and thanked him again. I told him I would call Du Plessis.

I did that at once. "Milo March," I said when he came on the phone. "I just wanted to thank you for your cooperation. Mr. Wilkins did a splendid job for me. I'm grateful to both of you."

"We are glad that we could be of service to you," he said. "If we can assist you in any way with the extradition work, please feel free to call on us."

"I'll do that. By the way, you might be interested to know

that I shall include you and your company in my report." I didn't add that there would be more about Wilkins in it than about him.

"That is very kind of you." I could tell by his voice that this pleased him more than he would admit. I told him I'd probably see him soon and said good-bye.

I sat in the lobby while I went through the morning newspaper. Then I went back to the bar. Since Crown was staying in this hotel, it seemed the best place to run into him again. I wanted the meeting to be accidental, so the bar was the best place, but I switched from martinis to whiskey and water and drank those as slowly as I could.

There was no sign of him all afternoon. That night I dropped down for a while, but he wasn't there. The following day I spent most of the time in the bar, and again he didn't show. The bartender and I were getting to be old friends. The next day, however, I had some luck.

I returned to the bar at cocktail time. I stopped just inside the doorway until my eyes could adjust to the dim lighting. I saw Crown sitting at the end of the bar. There was an empty stool next to him. The bar was mostly full, so it would seem perfectly natural if I took that stool. I walked the length of the bar and sat down. I knew that Crown looked at me, but I paid no attention.

The bartender came over, and we exchanged a few remarks. Then I ordered a martini. He was just starting down to mix it when Crown pushed his glass forward and asked for another one. The bartender picked up the glass and went on his way.

He brought both drinks back at the same time, rang up the

checks, and placed them in front of us. "You two chaps," he said, "should know each other, seeing as you're both Americans and both staying in the hotel. Mr. Pare, Mr. March." It couldn't have been better.

I looked around, smiling, and held out my hand. "How are you, Mr. Pare?"

He shook hands with me. "Glad to meet you. Been here long?"

"Only a few days. I'd begun to think I was the only American in the city."

"Actually," he said, "while I am an American, I'm now a citizen of Holland. For work reasons. You here on business?"

I shook my head. "Vacation."

"I'm here looking for a job," he volunteered. "They make good money here. What do you do, Mr. March?"

"I work for an insurance company in New York City." Well, I was sticking to the truth so far. "You been here long?"

"About a week. Have you gone out on the town yet?"

"No. I've been catching up on my sleep. But I have read some of the newspapers and magazines, and I'm beginning to think that I came to the wrong place to relax. I haven't seen any of those pretty broads I saw in the travel folders."

This caught his interest. "You said it. I been around to all the nightclubs and bars, and I ain't seen a single broad you can even try to pick up. Maybe I'll change my mind about wanting to work here."

"I don't blame you. I think I should have gone to Paris."

"I'd like to go sometime," he said. He sounded wistful.

When our drinks were finished, I bought the next round.

Then he bought the one after that. We'd been talking most of the time about the United States and cities we'd been to and about broads. So I decided to push it a little farther and asked him if he'd like to have dinner with me. The invitation seemed to cheer him up, and he accepted. We finished those drinks and went into the dining room. We ordered another round of drinks and dinner.

"I guess you've traveled a lot," he said.

"Quite a bit."

"I'd like to travel," he said, and that wistful note was back. "You get tired of spending most of your life in one … one place." I think he had started to say something like "one cell" but had caught himself. I could imagine that was one of the toughest things he had to face, watching what he said. I had already noticed that he spoke slowly, as though watching every word. Of course, a prison was not the best place to learn acceptable social conversation.

"This is a funny place," he said. "I don't get it."

"What do you mean?"

"All these rules they got about different people. Like they got people they call coloreds. They're part white and part black. Back home we'd call them niggers, but it ain't that easy here. Some of them are as white as you and me, and they got good jobs. But you ain't supposed to have nothing to do with them. And I was told if I wanted a job here, I'd better stay away from them. Now, it figures that they didn't get that white just by staying out of the sun. Somebody must've been playing around under the blankets."

I laughed. "Let me tell you a story, Melford." We were using first names by this time. "It's about Cape Town, but it's true of all South Africa. The first Dutch ship to land here was commanded by a man named Jan van Riebeeck. There were thirty men and one woman on the ship. The woman was Mrs. Van Riebeeck. The story says that Jan van Riebeeck planted the gardens that you see outside this hotel, and his men planted the first coloreds. The white men who followed them have kept up the good work—with a certain amount of enthusiasm. But under the blankets, as you said."

He laughed. By the time we were through dinner, we were practically old friends. That night, and for the next two nights, we went out and visited various nightclubs. But we didn't make any friends or meet any broads. It was pretty much the way he, and Fred Wilkins, had described it.

We did the same thing the next two evenings and nights. In the meantime, I was beginning to get an idea. On the third day, I met him in the bar and to have lunch later. I waited until he had three drinks under his belt, then I brought up my idea.

"I was thinking about our problems last night, Mel," I said. "I have an idea. Why don't you and I catch a plane tomorrow and go to Paris for two or three days and have some fun? Then we can come back here and rest up. It's a great place for resting."

I could see that it got to him. "I don't know," he said slowly. I knew he was trying to weigh the temporary loss of security against the possible gains. "You know some broads in Paris?"

"Yes," I said. It wasn't exactly true, but I knew I could arrange to know some. "I make pretty good money, and you can go as my guest."

"I have enough money," he said. He seemed to be having an inner struggle, and I didn't push any stronger. Then he straightened up. "We'll do it. Two days. And nights."

"I'll make the reservations today, and we'll leave tomorrow."

"Okay." He'd made up his mind.

After lunch I went to make the reservations. He stood beside me while I made them. We would leave the next morning. He wanted to know if he should buy any clothes. I said that I didn't know what he had, but from what I'd seen he didn't need to. Then he asked about money, and I told him we could change our money to francs when we reached Paris. On the pretense that I needed to buy a couple of ties, I left him with the understanding that we would meet again that evening in the hotel.

I walked through the gardens, past the statues of Cecil Rhodes and General Smuts, the pink Parliament buildings (I wondered how they explained those),* into Adderley Street and then the Strand. I bought a couple of ties in case I ran into him on the way back. I found a place where I could make a phone call from a booth. I got the Paris rates from the operator and then enough change to make the call. I put in a call to Henri Flambeau in Paris. He was with the CIA there, and we had worked together many times.

Several minutes went by, and then I heard his familiar voice.

---

* Actually it was the Mount Nelson Hotel that was baby pink. Nicknamed the Pink Lady, it was painted pink for peace in 1918. Milo apparently missed this in his bafflement that the government building color wasn't more somber (and masculine?).

"Henri," I said, "this is Milo."

"Milo!" He shouted so loud I had to hold the receiver away from my ear. "Where are you, my friend?"

"Cape Town, South Africa."

"*Sacré bleu!* What are you doing there? Retiring from the world?"

"Not yet. I want to ask you a favor."

"Ask."

"I will be in Paris tomorrow. No, wait. I won't be able to see much of you. There will be a man with me. He is someone that I expect to take back to the States—more or less in chains. I want to get him where he can be extradited. I've talked him into flying to Paris with me for a night on the town. He doesn't know that I'm after him. First, I want you to give me the name of a good hotel. I don't want to go to anywhere I'm known."

"That is easy, *mon ami.* La Ronde Hotel. Any taxi driver will know where it is. Very chic, very expensive, you'll love it. What's the case?"

"I'll tell you some other time, not at international phone rates. Call the hotel and make reservations for two. Adjoining rooms. I don't want him to get too far out of my sight. And there's one more thing. The guy is crazy about broads."

"What's wrong with that?" he demanded indignantly. "So am I and so are you—or have you gotten too old?"

"He's different," I said patiently. "He's never had very many. They don't have them walking around in prisons. Fix us up with two broads for tomorrow night. He likes blondes. He's not a bad-looking guy and he's all right, but he's eager. Be sure it's a broad who will go to bed with him. It'll probably be his last chance for a while. Get me a brunette—just so I can tell which one is which. And get me one that won't scream if I leave her early. When I can, I'll drop her off and meet you for some late drinking."

"You flatter me, Milo. I never thought I'd find you turning down a woman to drink with me. You must be getting old."

"I just came here from Hong Kong, leaving what is probably the best woman in the whole world. Make the reservations at the hotel in the names of Milo March and Melford Pare." I spelled both the names for him. "And don't forget the girls."

"I already know who to get. The blonde is named Yvonne and the brunette is Chérie. I'll have them meet you at the New York Bar at eight o'clock."

"The brunette must be an American broad who wants everyone to think she's French," I said sourly. "As soon as it can be done, I'll ditch her and see you at home. Are the girls pros?"

"No—but it wouldn't hurt you to be gallant and give them a few francs. I will await your call, my friend."

I hung up and got the overtime charges from the operator. It was enough to let de Gaulle build another nuclear bomb.* On the way back to the hotel I picked up another carton of American cigarettes.

I continued down the Strand and turned into Adderley

---

* France developed its own nuclear technology despite American objections to President Charles de Gaulle's military ambitions. By 1968 France was already testing a hydrogen bomb. De Gaulle resigned the presidency in April 1969, and this Milo March book was published in February 1970; so this outdated reference must have escaped notice.

Street, looking in the shop windows and taking my time. I had almost reached Government Street when I got a shock.

Coming down the street, headed in my direction, was Whitey Smith.

FOURTEEN

He hadn't seen me, so I ducked into a store and bought a couple of things. Finally I went back to the front of the store, and he wasn't in sight. So I went on to the hotel, but keeping a sharp watch for him. He must have, I decided, bribed someone in the Hong Kong air terminal and found out where I had gone.

There was only one thing he could do here, and that was start checking all the hotels. It might take him several days to get to the Mount Nelson, and he might get there any minute. I doubted that he would recognize Crown if he saw him, and he didn't know the name that Crown was using. But he would recognize me if he saw me. I was glad we were going to Paris in the morning.

Back at the hotel, I went to my room. I put away the things I had bought and then sat down to think about the situation. The odds were against his finding out that I was in that particular hotel before we left. The flight was scheduled for early in the morning, and there were a lot of hotels in Cape Town. Good hotels. I'd see that we didn't go out that night.

I spent a couple of hours in the room and then went down to the bar. Crown was sitting there, nursing a drink. He brightened up as soon as he saw me.

"Get your shopping done?" he asked.

"Yeah," I said. I ordered two drinks for us and sat on the stool to the far side of him. That way I could see the entrance to the bar in the event that Whitey entered. I also had put the gun in my pocket for the same reason. "I did two other things while I was out. I made reservations for us at a hotel in Paris. Guess what else I did."

"What?" he asked. He sounded like a kid.

"We have dates tomorrow night in Paris with two broads. At the New York Bar. You've got a blonde. I've got a brunette."

"Sounds great," he said, trying to control the sound of excitement. "Can we make it with them?"

"No question about it. You've never been to Paris, have you?"

"No."

"Well, I want to tell you one thing. These broads are not pros. But when you leave yours, tell her that you wanted to bring her a present but you didn't have time. Then give her ten or twenty bucks and tell her to get something for herself. And, whether you like her or not, take her phone number and tell her you'll call her the next day. Then you either will or not, depending on how you feel."

"She won't be insulted?"

"Not if you put it that way. I'll also tell you an old saying that is true. First, these girls are not whores, but they are semi-whores, like a lot of broads back in the States. The saying is: Always treat a whore as if she were a lady, and always treat a lady as if she were a whore. Got it?"

"I think so," he said.

We had a few more drinks and finally went in to dinner. I

made sure that we had more drinks there and still more after we'd finished dinner. I finally got him drunk enough so there was no problem getting him to go to bed.

I had left a call, so I was up early that morning. I packed most of my things, leaving a few items so they wouldn't think I had left for good. I took my bag downstairs and went to the desk. I told the clerk that Mr. Pare and I were going on a two-day holiday and would be back. But to make sure that our rooms would be kept until we returned, I would pay our bills through the two days. He was very nice about it, but I insisted and paid him. Then I used the house phone and called Crown. He sounded hungover when he answered but brightened up as soon as I told him we had to catch a plane. I said I'd meet him in the dining room for breakfast.

We left for the airport immediately after breakfast. There was still no sign of Whitey, but I didn't relax until we were on the plane. It had been a short night, so I went to sleep almost as soon as the plane took off. I think Crown did, too.

After arriving in Paris, we took a taxi to the hotel. It was all that Henri had said it would be. And we had adjoining rooms with a door that opened between them. I phoned Henri when I got to the room. He said that everything was set with the girls and they'd be at the New York Bar at eight. If I didn't recognize them when they came in, they'd ask the bartender for me. I thanked him and told him I'd call later. I told Crown I was going to take a nap and went to bed.

I still had plenty of time when I awakened. I showered and shaved and got dressed. I looked into the next room, but Crown wasn't there. He'd probably gone out for his first look at Paris. I went downstairs to the bar and had a drink. Crown came in before I'd finished it. We had a drink while he told me what he'd seen and the things he'd bought.

We went to the New York Bar a little after seven-thirty. Instead of going to the bar, we took a table. We ordered drinks and talked while we waited. Crown was nervous.

They came in exactly at eight. They were both good-looking broads. The brunette was in front. I stood up and went to meet them. "Hello," I said. "I'm Milo March. You must be Chérie and your friend is Yvonne."

"Yes," the brunette said with a smile. I had spoken in English, and she answered in the same language.

The blonde smiled. "You are a friend of Henri's?"

"For many years," I said truthfully. "Come. We have a table."

I led them back to the table and introduced them to Crown. We sat down and ordered drinks. Both girls were expert at putting people at ease, and Crown was soon relaxed and talking with the blonde. We had several drinks there and then went on to a restaurant that had good food and a floor show. We had several drinks after dinner, and then we left, separating. Crown went with the blonde, and I took Chérie home.

On the way to her home, I made a point of telling her how much I enjoyed being with her and explained that I had to work but I would see her again soon. I took her phone number and told her that I might have to go back to America first but that I would call her soon. I meant it. I also took her handbag, admiring it, and put a fifty-dollar bill in it. I escorted her to her door, the taxi waiting, then went on to Henri's apartment.

It was good to see him again. We sat around drinking brandy and talking. I kept a watch on the time, and when it was five in the morning I asked Henri if I could use his phone. He nodded. I put a call in to Martin Raymond at home in New York City. It was eleven at night there.

"Where are you calling from, Milo?" he said when he answered. "Cape Town?"

"Paris."

"What the hell are you doing in Paris?"

"I've got Eugene Crown here."

There was a moment of silence. "I knew you'd come through," he exclaimed then. "I knew that you could do it. I put myself on the block with the board. ... How come Paris? I thought you said he was in Cape Town."

"He was. But there's a little problem there about extradition. So I talked him into coming with me on a holiday."

"Great. I'm proud of you, my boy."

"Forget that bit," I said. "Just make sure that my name is spelled right on the bonus check and that it's large enough."

"Don't worry about that, Milo. I'll take care of you. I'll get in touch with the authorities."

"There's just one thing, Martin," I said. "It is now shortly after five in the morning in Paris. I want to have until noon. I've got him, but I don't have all the information I need. So I don't want any cops coming around before noon today. You can phone the FBI and tell them I have him but that I'm calling you back to tell you where. And don't rub it in. They are a little annoyed at me as it is. Be humble—even if it is foreign to your nature. Just tell them that while working on another case, I stumbled into him. As a good citizen I will keep him occupied until they come to get him. But I need at least six hours. Then you can call them back and tell them I'm at La Ronde Hotel in Paris, room seven-two-three. Crown will be with me. When you've done that, call me at the hotel."

"All right, Milo," he said. He was already beginning to sound humble. Martin was a natural method actor. He didn't have to imagine he felt it; he did feel it. "This is a proud day for all of us."

"Sure," I said sourly. "Just remember to spell my name right on the check." I hung up.

"Do you always treat your employers that way?" Henri asked.

"Sure," I said. "That's the secret of my charm."

"I wondered what it was," he said, and we both laughed.

We had another drink together, and then I left. I went back to the hotel and looked into the adjoining room. Crown was asleep. There was a pleased expression on his face, so I guessed that he'd had a pleasant night. I was glad. It would probably be a long time before he had another one.

I sat in the room for a time, thinking about the rest of the day. I had to plan what was going to happen. I realized that I didn't want Eugene Crown merely thrown into chains and dragged off—any more than I had wanted Whitey Smith to kill him.

Finally I went downstairs and had some breakfast. I bought a bottle, left word for some ice to be delivered, and went back to my room. I poured a drink and read the newspaper I had picked up.

Crown got up about ten o'clock. I heard him taking a shower, and a few minutes later he knocked on my door. I told him to come in. He looked slightly hungover but happy.

"What time did you get back?" he asked.

"About six," I said. "Pour yourself a drink and I'll order some breakfast for you. What do you want?"

He told me, and I phoned the order to room service. I went to my bag and got the gun from the false bottom and put it in my pocket. He didn't see what I was doing. I went back and sat down while he attacked the breakfast. A few minutes later the phone rang. I picked up the receiver and said hello.

It was Martin Raymond. "Milo, I just talked to the FBI. They'll have a man there, with a French detective, in about two hours. Is that all right?"

"That's fine."

"You'll leave Paris today?"

"Yeah."

"He's with you now?"

"Yeah."

"Well, I'll see you sometime tomorrow, eh?"

"I don't think so. But I'll call you."

"All right. I'll talk to you. Good work, boy."

Crown looked up as I put the receiver down. "A friend of yours?"

"Not quite. That was my boss in New York City. I can't even take a vacation without him calling to check."

"Tough," he said, but I could tell his mind wasn't with it. "Say, that was a great broad you got for me. She's really something. I got her phone number, and I'm going to see her again tonight."

This was the time for it. I took a deep breath. "I'm afraid that you won't be able to see her tonight … Eugene."

It took a minute for it to soak in. When it did, he looked frightened. But only for a minute. Then the expression was replaced by one of caution. His new image must have done him some good. "You a cop?" he asked.

"No. I work for an insurance company, like I told you. They aren't making anything out of it, but they are paying me to find out what really happened in Cleveland and to find you. I've done the latter. I have a pretty good idea about the first, and I'll dig up the rest of it. The FBI and a French detective will be here in two hours. I want to talk to you while we wait."

"About what? What if I don't want to talk? What if I just get up and walk out?"

"I have a gun," I said gently. I showed it to him. "And I want to say one other thing immediately. I don't believe that you killed Randolph. I do believe you were involved, but that's not the same charge. You know Whitey Smith, don't you?"

"What if I do?" he asked bitterly.

"Whitey Smith is a killer. He's been looking for you. A few nights ago he tried to kill Joe Capo. He didn't succeed, but he wounded Capo badly. Capo is in hiding somewhere. Whitey has been following me. I thought I had lost him in Hong Kong, but yesterday I saw him in Cape Town. He didn't see me. But you can't run forever, Eugene. Whitey will eventually find you. Or the FBI will eventually do the same thing. Sure, you won't go completely free. You'll have to serve a number of years. With the changes you've already made in yourself, it might not be too many years, especially if you cooperate with the prosecution. And that will be better than ending up on a slab."

"How'd you find me when they couldn't?"

"Because I didn't use the same approach they did. I found out what sort of person you were. I talked to your brother and to the prison psychologist—and to Rhoda Ames."

That startled him. "You talked to her? What did she say?"

"She hoped that you could be helped. She seemed to think that I wanted to help you and could."

"How did you know about her?"

"Your brother told me."

"Ben? He's a good guy. He was always smarter than me. How come he talked that much to you?"

"Because I wasn't asking the same questions and didn't have the same attitude as the others. He wanted to see you live. So did Rhoda. So do I."

"You got a gun," he said, "so I can't run. Go ahead and talk. But I got to tell you one thing. I don't believe that Whitey would kill me. If anything happened to me, Whitey and a lot of other guys would be in trouble. I left evidence with a friend of mine. If he doesn't hear from me every month, he sends the stuff to the cops. That'll keep Whitey off my back."

"Then why is he in Cape Town? Smarten up, Eugene. So you gave some notes to Bernie Shale in Reno. So what you wrote might make a few stories in the newspapers, but it would blow over. Who's going to believe an escaped con or an ex-con? And if Whitey ever found Bernie, you can bet that he'd make Bernie fold up."

"Bernie told you?" he asked.

I shook my head. "He didn't have to. I saw Bernie, but I didn't talk to him. I saw him get a letter with money in it from Lisbon. I didn't have to have it spelled out for me. It was Bernie who also told you where to go for a forged passport in San Francisco. Anyone can figure that out once they know a few things. Even the FBI may stumble on it any day. And they'll make Bernie fold, too."

"I don't get it. What's your scam?"

"My scam is that I'm trying to save your life. I don't think you deserve to be killed—legally or otherwise. The first thing is to see that you get a trial instead of a bullet. I'll see that you get a lawyer. A good one. I'll see that you get other help. If I can find him, I wouldn't be surprised if Joe Capo ends up as a witness to help take you off the hook."

"You mean that?"

"Your brother thinks I mean it and so does Rhoda Ames."

He was silent for a minute. "Why'd you get me to come to Paris with you?"

"First, because there would be trouble about extradition from South Africa, and I didn't want to see you spending months in one of their crummy jails. Then, I thought you deserved at least one night on the town."

He thought for a minute. "That was really some broad. I wish I could see her again tonight." He looked at me sharply. "Level with me. What do you think my chances are?"

"As good as you can expect," I said. "You'll have to go back to prison no matter what happens. But it's better than having a lot of marble setting on your head. I think you'll beat this rap except for the conspiracy charge. I said I'll get you a good lawyer. You won't have to pay him anything. And I'll find Joe Capo one way or another and make him testify for you. He'd rather stay alive, too. And I'll see that the information you left with Bernie goes into court, too."

"What happens to Bernie?"

"Nothing. If I can get him to turn the paper over to me, I'll forget I ever heard of him. And I'll do one more thing. How much were you sending Bernie?"

"Two hundred a month for as long as I stayed alive and free."

"I'll see that he gets it for at least another six months."

He took a deep breath and let it out slowly. "Okay, Milo. Outside of my brother and maybe Rhoda, you're the only person who's ever leveled with me. What do you want to know?"

"Everything. Who shot Randolph?"

"I wasn't there, but I'm sure that Whitey did. He rented the apartment for me. Then I had to move in with the gun that I bought in Texas. I was told to leave my car there and to buy another one in Cleveland. I left my car, but I took a plane to Columbus and bought a car there instead. I drove it as far as Illinois and sold it and took a plane."

"You had help getting out of the joint in Columbus?"

"Yeah. I did time with Joe Capo, and he came to see me. He would help me get out, and I was to do whatever he told me and they'd give me money. I knew right away that I was being set up for a fall guy, but I figured if I got enough bread I could make it."

I nodded. "Ben told me you could smell a trap."

He smiled. "Ben always said that. Maybe he was right. I knew that's what it was, but Joe was talking about a lot of money, and I needed money to do what I wanted. So I agreed."

"How much money did they pay you?"

"About fifty thousand. They didn't plan on that much. But at the end, after Cleveland, I demanded twenty-five thousand and told them what I had stashed. So I got it."

"I thought that was the way it went. What about the other people that were in it?"

"I never knew anybody but Joe and Whitey," he said. "But I followed Joe one time. I'd figured he was the contact man. There was a meeting at a house in Texas. A big house. I don't know the names of the other people, but I have a complete description of all of them. And I have the license plate numbers of the cars they arrived in and the address of the house where they met."

"Smart," I said. "Bernie Shale has that. Right?"

"Yeah. In a safe deposit box."

"Why did they want to kill Randolph?"

"I don't know," he said simply. "I didn't know that anyone was going to be killed until they had me buy the rifle and take it to that apartment. I didn't know who it was until I read it in the papers. They took me for a pigeon, so I figured that let me take them for anything I could."

"I don't blame you," I said. "I would have done the same

thing. Look, Gene, you'll have to do some more time. Sure, you'll lose a few years, but it's better than losing all of them. And I think you've learned enough to manage to get out in a few years. I'll have the lawyer for you before you're back in the States. All I have to do is find Joe Capo and get the paper from Bernie."

Again he took a moment. "I can help," he said finally. "I can tell you where you can probably find Joe. And I can make it certain that you get the goods from Bernie if you swear that his name will not come into it."

"I swear," I said.

"You know a town in Arizona called Kingman?"

"Yeah."

"There's a wide place in the road some miles outside of Kingman that's called Chloride.* I tailed Joe to it once. He owns a little yellow house there. I don't think there's an address on it, but it's the only yellow house in town. When he wants to hide out that's where he goes. There he's known as Joe Capella, and the people think he's a salesman."

"I'll find him."

"Joe and me were cellmates once in a joint, and I never thought he'd play me for a patsy. But he did. Me and Bernie were cellmates once, too. Several years ago. But I always remembered two things about him. He used to talk to me about the time when he was making it big, and I remembered that he used to live in Reno when he wasn't doing a job, and that once he told me about getting a forged passport

* Chloride is a historical silver mining town of the Old West. It has only a few hundred residents but has attracted thousands of tourists due to its "ghost town" status.

in San Francisco. So after Joe came to see me in the joint, I wrote a letter to Bernie and mailed it to Reno—to a bar there. He sent me an answer through the same guy that smuggled my letter out. I knew I was getting enough dough from Joe to get my face operated on, so I started planning right then. I knew that was going to be my big chance. … Now I'll write the letter for you."

"There's a paper and a pen in the drawer right next to you."

He took out a sheet of paper and the pen and began to write. He stopped and looked up. "Is Milo your real name?"

"Yeah. Milo March."

He went back to writing. Finally he finished and put the pen down. "Want to read it?" he asked.

"No. Put it in an envelope and then put it in the drawer. Seal the envelope."

He looked at me. "I could have told Bernie to see that you got rubbed out."

"You could have," I admitted. "But it's your letter. Seal it. I don't go around reading mail that isn't mine." He scribbled another line on the page, then folded it and put it in an envelope and sealed it. He threw it in the drawer.

"Want a drink?" I asked.

"I could use one."

"Help yourself. There's ice in the bucket."

He poured a stiff drink and sat down again. "I'd like to ask you to do a favor for me."

"Anything. If I can do it, I will."

"Call Yvonne and tell her I can't see her tonight. But call her after I'm gone. Get her address and tell her I'll write her.

She's a real nice broad. Maybe I can come back and see her in twenty years or so."

"You won't have to do that much," I told him. "This time I think you'll be able to make parole. I'll get her address to you. Tell me one thing. Where the hell did you get all those fancy names you've been using?"

He grinned. "That's one thing I learned the first time I busted out of a joint. The biggest problem is to be able to remember the name you're using. So you pick names like that, and they're easier to remember than if you called yourself John Smith."

"It makes sense," I admitted. "I don't know how long extradition will take here, but I'll be back before you go. I'll have the lawyer ready, and he'll see you as soon as they bring you in. I'll also see that Capo and Whitey are delivered and that the paper Bernie has reaches the lawyer, too."

"Okay," he said. He lifted his glass in a silent toast and drank. "I guess maybe you're right about this being the best way. Things didn't quite work out the way I thought they would. I guess maybe I didn't look at it, but I knew that Whitey, or someone like him, would always be after me and I'd always be running. And I didn't have any of the fun I expected to have—except for last night. Will you do two more things for me?"

"Sure."

"Call my brother and ... call Rhoda."

"As soon as I get there."

He poured himself another drink and talked. Mostly about what life had been and what he had always wanted it to be.

Finally there was a knock on the door. I waited as he finished his drink and then opened the door. There were two men standing there. They each looked like what they were. An American cop and a French cop.

The one in front already had his ID out. "Hall," he said. "FBI. Are you March?"

"I'm March," I said.

"This is Detective Yves."

"Welcome, gentlemen," I said. "Come in. May I introduce Mr. Crown. Incidentally, he is voluntarily giving himself into your gentle care, so you won't need to take him out in cuffs."

The French detective smiled at me, but the FBI man scowled. "We'll decide about that," he said crisply.

"I'm sure you will," I said gently. "Now, I'd like to request one favor, Mr. Hall."

"What?" he asked suspiciously.

"When you meet with any newspapermen—which I'm sure you will—I'd be grateful if you did not mention my name in any way. I want no credit anywhere."

He looked surprised. "Why?"

"Publicity," I said, "is the death of any insurance investigator."

"All right," he said. He tried to make it sound as if he were doing me a favor, but he couldn't entirely conceal his own pleasure.

I went over and shook hands with Crown and told him I'd see him soon. He smiled and nodded. Then I stood and watched them take him out. I felt sadness, and I realized that I was very tired. And it was not because of lack of sleep.

I phoned the blond girl and gave her a plausible story and got her address. Then I phoned the airport and got a reservation on the first plane for New York City.

FIFTEEN

When I arrived at Kennedy Airport in New York City, the first thing I did was call Martin Raymond. He came on at once.

"Milo, boy, where are you?" he asked.

"Kennedy Airport."

"Everything go all right?"

"Yeah. An FBI man named Hall and a French cop picked up Crown. Everything is just fine."

"You'll be in soon?"

"No. You asked me to do two things. Find Crown and solve what happened in Cleveland. I've only done the first. I'm taking a plane out of here as soon as I can get it."

"You've got a lead?"

"Yeah. I'll be in touch with you, Martin." I hung up.

Next I phoned a lawyer I knew. His name was Harrison Lee, and he was one of the best defense attorneys in the country. I told him the facts about the case and added that I would have more ammunition for him within the next day or two. He said he would take the case and would talk to Crown as soon as he was permitted to do so. I told him to bill Intercontinental Insurance. We ended the conversation with me promising to call him within twenty-four hours.

I went out and got a ticket that would get me to Kingman, Arizona. Then I made more calls. One was to Ben Crown in

Columbus, Ohio, and the other was to Rhoda Ames in Athens, Ohio. And the other two were to a newspaperman in Washington and one in Cleveland.

I boarded the plane and slept most of the way to Kingman. When I arrived there, I rented a car and asked for directions to Chloride. I had no trouble finding the house. It was the only yellow house in town. I parked and went up and knocked on the door.

I could hear someone moving around in the house, but it was a couple of minutes before I got more than that. Then a voice came through the closed door. "Who is it?"

"A friend," I said. "I just came from Gene Crown. And I know where Whitey is. I want to talk to you."

There was a moment of silence, then the click of the lock. "All right," he said. "Come in, but carefully."

I opened the door and stepped inside, closing the door behind me. Joe Capo was standing in the middle of the room, a gun in one hand. His other arm was in a sling, and there was still a bandage on his neck. He hadn't shaved, and he looked as if he hadn't slept.

"Who are you?" he asked.

"My name is Milo March. I left Gene Crown in Paris, but the FBI is bringing him back here to face trial. I have also arranged for a lawyer to represent him. Day before yesterday, Whitey Smith was in Cape Town, South Africa. I imagine he will be back here before long."

He waved the gun at me. "Go in the kitchen and sit down."

I went into the next room and sat at the kitchen table. The sink was full of dirty dishes, and there was a bottle of whiskey on the table. He sat across from me, still holding the gun. "Let's hear your story," he said.

"May I have a drink?" I asked. "I just got off a plane."

"Help yourself."

I found a clean glass and poured a drink over ice. I sat down across from him and lit a cigarette.

"It's a short story," I said. "You've got a hideout here, but how long do you think it's safe? The FBI will be looking and so will Whitey. You were the contact man in a conspiracy to commit an assassination. The law wants you because they need you. The killers, like Whitey, want to shut your mouth. You can't avoid both of them forever."

"How did you find out where I was?"

"Crown. He followed you a couple of times. Once to this house and once to a house in Texas. In that case, he wrote down the address and a description of everyone who arrived that night at the house and the numbers of the license plates of the cars that brought them."

He cursed and took another drink. "You got an idea, bright boy?"

"Yeah. If you're smart, you'll agree to testify for the state and be held under protective arrest. You can probably make a deal."

"What chance do you think I'd have then?"

"More than you have now, Joe. You remember something Joe Louis once said about the ring? You can run but you can't hide.* It applies to your case, too. If you don't get them first, Whitey, or someone like him, will one day look at you over

* According to legend, heavyweight king Joe Louis's comment was made before his historic June 1941 fight with light-heavyweight champ Billy Conn, in reference to Conn's quick footwork: "He can run but he can't hide."

the top of the sights of a gun. There is no appeal from that kind of thing."

He stared gloomily at his drink. "You got an idea?"

"Yeah. I got a lawyer for Crown. Did you ever hear of Harrison Lee?"

"Sure. He's a great mouthpiece. What about him?"

"He's representing Crown. Through him we can make a deal with the prosecutor. He'll keep you under protective custody so no one can kill you. You tell him what you know, and you may also get a deal that gives you immunity. At least you'll be alive."

"For how long?" he asked bitterly.

"Longer than you will be if you don't do it. You and Crown and I know that Whitey killed Randolph and that the three of you were paid to do it by a group of men with a lot of money. Do you want them to go free while you fry?"

"I know," he said angrily. "Do you believe I haven't thought about it? Are you saying you can arrange that?"

"I am. All I have to do is make a phone call and wait for a call back. If you tell me to make the call, I'll stay with you until you're in protective custody. I've also got a gun out in my car, and I'll get it if you say it's all right." He was silent for a minute, and I could see the results of the inner struggle that was going on. Finally he raised his head and looked at me. I could tell that I had won.

"Make the call," he said. "Then we'll see."

"Okay," I said. I finished my drink and went into the living room, where I'd seen the phone. I put in a call to Harrison Lee. It was taken by a girl who said he was in Cleveland and gave me a number there. I called him at that number. It took a couple of minutes, but I finally got him.

I explained the situation to him, and he said he'd talk to the prosecutor and call me back. He'd had a short talk with Crown and expected to spend more time with him the next day. I gave him the number and hung up.

"He'll call back as soon as he can talk to the prosecutor," I told Capo. I poured myself another drink.

"What are you getting out of this?" he asked.

"Three hundred dollars a day and expenses," I said. "Besides, I like Crown and think he ought to get a break."

"What about me?"

"I don't know you—but I think you ought to get a break, too. I think that the guys who paid for this should get up on the firing line. If they're going to pay for something, let them pay all the way."

"Yeah," he grunted. "I buy that."

"Want me to get my gun?" I asked.

He thought about it for a minute. "I guess so," he said wearily. "It'll be better with two guns than just one."

I went out to the car and took the gun from beneath the false bottom of my bag. I went back into the house and put the gun on the table, and poured myself a drink.

"Now all we do is wait," I said.

It was almost an hour before the phone rang. He jumped as if he'd heard a shot. "That's probably for me," I said. I went to the phone and picked it up. It was the lawyer.

"The district attorney agrees to the plan. There will be two Federal agents there in less than two hours to pick up Capo."

"Okay," I said. "I'll be in touch."

I went back to the kitchen table. "It's a deal," I told him. "There will be two Federal agents here in less than two hours to take you back."

"Great," he said. "I don't like it, but I guess it's the only way. That Whitey bothers me. Can I trust that D.A.?"

"I think so. He has more to gain by keeping his word than by breaking it."

So we sat and smoked and drank. The bottle was just about finished when a car stopped in front of the house, and then there was a knock on the door. I slipped my gun in my pocket and went to open the door. There were two of them, and they dutifully displayed their identification cards. Then they arrested Capo as a witness.

"You're March?" one of them said to me as they were starting to leave.

"I'm March," I said.

"You seem to get around, don't you? I heard you were in Paris yesterday."

"You did? I thought you were from the FBI, not the FCC."

I watched them drive off with Capo, and then I got in my car and headed for Reno. I drove up north of Vegas, crossed into California, and hit Route 395 just below Bishop. I drove straight to Reno. When I crossed back into Nevada, I did something I'd forgotten on my last trip. I took my gun out of my pocket and put it on the seat. I reached Reno early in the morning. I registered at the Holiday Hotel at once. I'd had plenty of sleep on planes, so I walked down to Second Street. Jack Kenny was working.

"Hi," I said as he brought me a drink. "How are things?"

"Okay. Where have you been?"

"You really want to know? I'll tell you. San Francisco, Los Angeles, New York City, Lisbon, Hong Kong, Cape Town, Paris, New York City, Kingman, Arizona, and back to Reno."

"Sorry I asked," he said, laughing.

"Do you think Bernie Shale will be in this morning?"

"Should be. About ten o'clock. He's still got money, so I imagine he'll be here. Did you find the guy you were looking for?"

"I found him. What are you doing tonight?"

"Nothing. Why?"

"We'll go out on the town and I'll tell you the whole story. About eight o'clock?"

"Okay. I'll meet you here."

"I'll be here. I need to relax. I'll tell you about it while I'm relaxing."

He nodded and went off to wait on more customers. I sipped my drink and waited.

It was just about ten when Bernie Shale came in. He took a seat down in the middle of the bar. I caught Kenny's eyes and motioned for him to come up. He walked up and took a bottle of beer from the cabinet back of him. He stopped beside me.

"Tell him I want to buy the drink for him, but I want him to come here and sit with me so I can talk to him."

He nodded and went back to the little guy. They exchanged a few words, then Kenny brought the beer and a glass up and put them next to me and took my money. The little guy shambled up and sat on the stool next to me. He poured beer in the glass and looked at me.

"Thanks," he said. "Fuzz?"

"Not fuzz," I said. "I just came from a friend of yours. He sent a letter." I handed it to him and ignored everything until he'd finished reading it.

He put the letter back in the envelope and put it in his pocket. Then he looked at me. "You know what's in the letter?"

"I haven't seen it, but I know the general idea of it."

"Wait until I finish my beer," he said. "Then we'll go get it. What are his chances?"

"Pretty good, I think," I said. "I got a good lawyer for him, and there are several things going for him. I also got a witness for him that should clear him of a lot of things. He'll still have to do some time, but that's better than the Big Jump or taking a bum rap of any kind."

He took another pull on the beer. "What about me?"

"I never heard of you or saw you," I said. "You had an agreement with him. It'll still go on for the next six months."

"How and where?"

"Here. Kenny will have it for you the first of the month for six months."

He finished the beer. "Let's go."

I followed him out of the door and into the bank across the street. He went back to the safe deposit department and came back within a few minutes. We went outside and he handed me an envelope. We went back to the bar. I bought him a drink and gave Kenny ten dollars for further drinks and said I'd give him other things for him to keep and give out as indicated.

I left and went back to the hotel. First, I made out six envelopes to Bernie Shale and put a date on each one. I slipped two hundred dollars into each envelope and sealed them. Then I opened the envelope Bernie had given me. It was a tidy message. It contained exactly what he had said it would. There was an address in Texas, and there were the license numbers of four cars that four men had driven when they arrived at that house. The numbers indicated that they were rentals, so I got on a phone and did some checking.

I ended up with four names. I'd never met them, but I'd heard of most of them. One was from Texas, one from Louisiana, one from Chicago, and one from New York. Three of them were very rich. One wasn't, but was known for his political beliefs. The funny thing about them was that they didn't all really believe the same things. But they did all agree on one idea. Stir things up. Let there be riots and killings, and then they could get the things they want. A little for me and a little for you. Put the blame on the Communists, the Fascists, the blacks, the whites, but scare everybody and then we can make time, baby. They made me sick.

I put the names and Crown's notes into an envelope with a brief note to the lawyer, and addressed the letter to the lawyer and marked it *Air Mail, Special Delivery* and *Registered*. Then I called downstairs and had a boy come and pick it up. Then I left a call with the operator and went to sleep.

I got up just in time to make it. I went to Second Street, and Kenny was already there. So we started there. Then we moved to Harrah's and Harold's, just to show we had class, then to the Peppermint Lounge, where we drank and talked to Tommy. From there we moved to the Swiss Chalet on Mill

Street. I suddenly met more people than I had ever seen in such a short period of time. I met Dave, who owned the joint, and Vi, who should have, Cal and Diana, Jack, Bob, Rick, Bobby, Gary, Chip, and fifty others. All nice people.

All I really remember is that I was sitting at a table, in front of the fireplace, and talking to Kenny. I had already told him about the case, but I had one thing more to say. It took a little time to get it out.

"I have to tell you one thing," I finally said through a sort of haze. "You really have to say something for John Randolph. He was all things to all men. He was assassinated. This immediately put him into a special category. People who normally wouldn't even speak to each other were suddenly bonded together. Normally, there is someone who cares for the slain warrior—but with John Randolph there was always going to be somebody who would keep his grave green. And it should be so with anyone who is assassinated. Long may their place in the earth be verdant."

SIXTEEN

It wasn't easy, but I was up early the next morning. I had breakfast and was on my way to Los Angeles. I reached there about noon. I didn't bother to make a reservation in a hotel. I called International Airport and got passage on a plane for New York City that night. Then I went to see Bo. I told him the story. When it was time, I went to get my plane, leaving the rental car at International Airport.

It was morning when I arrived in New York City. By this time I didn't know what time it was or what day. I went to my apartment and left my suitcase, then took a taxi to Intercontinental. I went in to see good old Martin Raymond.

I told him the story, including every little thing. He was glad to see me. He also had two checks for me. One was a bonus check for five thousand dollars, and one was for my per-diem charge up to date. It was a nice figure, too.

"A great job, Milo, my boy," he said. "Great. This is to show our appreciation."

"Sure," I said. "Incidentally, I have already told the defense attorney to bill you for his charges."

"What?" he screamed. "We have to pay that?"

"You're not thinking, Martin," I said. "Remember, we're doing a public service. You've already taken ads saying that we were going to solve the case. Well, we've solved it. Now, we have paid all this money to prove what happened, and we say that Eugene Crown is not guilty and we offer our proof that Eugene Crown is no more than a pawn in this game of death. And this will prove that you are an insurance company with a heart."

He was silent for a minute. "Milo, my boy," he said enthusiastically, "that's a great idea. I wish I'd thought of it."

"You will, Martin," I said wearily. "May I go now?"

That stopped him for a minute. "Yes. Of course you may. We have nothing pending at the moment. Why don't you take a vacation, Milo? You have earned it."

"You may have an idea," I said. "I'll send you the report and the expense account."

"Take your time," he said grandly. "We'll be in touch."

"I'm sure," I said.

I walked out, went downstairs, and cashed the checks. I went home to my apartment. My answering service had no messages that were important. I sat down and thought about the problem for ten minutes. Then I went to the telephone and made a reservation for the next plane to Hong Kong.

AFTERWORD

Stir Things Up

Whenever an Author's Note claims that all the characters portrayed in this novel are fictional and are not meant to represent anyone living or dead, you naturally wonder who and what the novel is really about, or at least what inspired it. In *Green Grow the Graves,* a prominent congressman is assassinated, the suspect firing the murder weapon from a fourth-story window. A sinister figure, a gun for the mob, pursues the suspect, determined to kill him. Conspiracy theories, anyone?

Milo observes: "This was our fourth political assassination—fifth if you counted the killing of the man accused of committing one of them—in less than six years."

Let's see, *Green Grow the Graves* was published in February 1970, and I assume the manuscript was completed in early 1969, or even earlier (the process of publishing a book commercially can take a year or more). Ergo, the story probably takes place around 1968–1969, especially judging by the comment about France's President de Gaulle as if he were still in office (he left office in April 1969). So between 1963 and 1969, three major previous political assassinations were of President John F. Kennedy (November 1963), Reverend

Martin Luther King, Jr. (April 1968), and Senator Robert F. Kennedy (June 1968).* And of course Lee Harvey Oswald was the accused assassin of JFK, who was in turn assassinated by Jack Ruby in November 1963.

Isn't it odd that in a book that alludes to the Kennedy assassination and the murder of the assassin, the fictional congressman John Randolph is so Kennedy-like, a wealthy man from a family of public servants, killed by a shooter from an upper story of a nearby building, and the suspect himself becomes the target of an underworld figure? I'm reminded of the Milo March novel of 1956, *A Lonely Walk,* which is based on the famous Wilma Montesi murder case of 1953, yet that real case is mentioned in the book as if the fictional murder didn't closely resemble it. Authorial humor?

Milo March seeks proof that the suspected assassin, Eugene Crown, is no more than a pawn of a well-organized international conspiracy. Milo eventually ends up with four names: "I'd never met them, but I'd heard of most of them. One was from Texas, one from Louisiana, one from Chicago, and one from New York. Three of them were very rich. One wasn't, but was known for his political beliefs. The funny thing about them was that they didn't all really believe the same things. But they did all agree on one idea. Stir things up. Let there be riots and killings, and then they could get the things they want. A little for me and a little for you. Put the blame on the Communists, the Fascists, the blacks, the whites, but scare everybody and then we can make time, baby. They made me sick."

* Not counted are the murders of Malcolm X in 1965 and George Lincoln Rockwell, leader of the American Nazi Party, in 1967, though those were arguably political assassinations.

The author, Ken Crossen, felt sick about something, I can tell. Throughout the series, he uses Milo as his mouthpiece for various gripes (culminating in the final novel, *Death to the Brides,* in which Ken, I mean Milo, gets to curse out the President of the United States himself). But I don't know enough about the history of conspiracy theories to read what is behind Milo's words, and whether he had actual identities in mind.

Maybe Milo is hinting at a conspiracy theory of Ken's. Or maybe "only the climate of violence is real" in the story, "in a world which has seen too much of it over the centuries."

Kendra Crossen Burroughs

ABOUT THE AUTHOR

Kendell Foster Crossen (1910–1981), the only child of Samuel Richard Crossen and Clo Foster Crossen, was born on a farm outside Albany in Athens County, Ohio—a village of some 550 souls in the year of this birth. His ancestors on his mother's side include the 19th-century songwriter Stephen Collins Foster ("Oh! Susanna"); William Allen, founder of Allentown, Pennsylvania; and Ebenezer Foster, one of the Minute Men who sprang to arms at the Lexington alarm in April 1775.

Ken went to Rio Grande College on a football scholarship but stayed only one year. "When I was fairly young, I developed the disgusting habit of reading," says Milo March, and it seems Ken Crossen, too, preferred self-education. He loved literature and poetry; favorite authors included Christopher Marlowe and Robert Service. He also enjoyed participant sports and was a semi-pro fighter in the heavyweight class. He became a practicing magician and had a passion for chess.

After college Ken wrote several one-act plays that were produced in a small Cleveland theater. He worked in steel mills and Fisher Body plants. Then he was employed as an insurance investigator, or "claims adjuster," in Cleveland. But he left the job and returned to the theater, now as a performer: a tumbling clown in the Tom Mix Circus; a comic and carnival barker for a tent show, and an actor in a medicine show.

In 1935, Ken hitchhiked to New York City with a typewriter under his arm, and found work with the WPA Writers' Project, covering cricket for the *New York City Guidebook*. In 1936, he was hired by the Munsey Publishing Company as associate editor of the popular *Detective Fiction Weekly*. The company asked him to come up with a character to compete with The Shadow, and thus was born a unique superhero of pulps, comic books, and radio—The Green Lama, an American mystic trained in Tibetan Buddhism.

Crossen sold his first story, "The Aaron Burr Murder Case," to *Detective Fiction Weekly* in September 1939, but says he didn't begin to make a living from writing till 1941. He tried his hand at publishing true crime magazines, comics, and a picture magazine, without great success, so he set out for Hollywood. From his typewriter flowed hundreds of stories, short novels for magazines, scripts radio, television, and film, nonfiction articles. He delved into science fiction in the 1950s, starting with "Restricted Clientele" (February 1951). His dystopian novels *Year of Consent* and *The Rest Must Die* also appeared in this decade.

In the course of his career Ken Crossen acquired six pseud-onyms: Richard Foster, Bennett Barlay, Kent Richards, Clay Richards, Christopher Monig, and M.E. Chaber. The variety was necessary because different publishers wanted to reserve specific bylines for their own publications. Ken based "M.E. Chaber" on the Hebrew word for "author," *mechaber.*

In the early '50s, as M.E. Chaber, Crossen began to write a series of full-length mystery/espionage novels featuring Milo March, an insurance investigator. The first, *Hangman's Harvest,* was published in 1952. In all, there are twenty-two Milo March novels. One, *The Man Inside,* was made into a British film starring Jack Palance.

Most of Ken's characters were private detectives, and Milo was the most popular. Paperback Library reissued twenty-five Crossen titles in 1970–1971, with covers by Robert McGin-nis. Twenty were Milo March novels, four featured an insur-ance investigator named Brian Brett, and one was about CIA agent Kim Locke.

Crossen excelled at producing well-plotted entertainment with fast-moving action. His research skills were a strong asset, back when research meant long hours searching library microfilms and poring over street maps and hotel floorplans. His imagination took him to many international hot spots, although he himself never traveled abroad. Like Milo March, he hated flying ("When you've seen one cloud, you've seen them all").

Ken Crossen was married four times. With his first wife he had three children (Stephen, Karen, Kendra) and with his second a son (David). He lived in New York, Florida, Southern California, Nevada, and other parts of the country. Milo March moves from Denver to New York City after five books of the series, with an apartment on Perry Street in Greenwich Village; that's where Ken lived, too. His and Milo's favorite watering hole was the Blue Mill Tavern, a short walk from the apartment.

Ken Crossen was a combination of many of the traits of his different male characters: tough, adventuresome, with a taste for gin and shapely women. But perhaps the best observation was made in an obituary written by sci-fi writer Avram Davidson, who described Ken as a fundamentally gentle person who had been buffeted by many winds.

CPSIA information can be obtained
at www.ICGtesting.com
Printed in the USA
FSHW010641200521
81527FS